It took me ages to get to sleep. I'd jump awake thinking the ghost was in my room. Then I dreamt it had turned into a bat, swooping down on me out of the darkness. I even saw its fangs. I yelled and woke myself up.

What a relief. Except when I opened my eyes it was pitch dark. That really thick blackness, like a great fog. I hate waking up at this time. I tried to snuggle down into bed. I was just closing my eyes when I heard somthing.

Someone was calling me.

It was a dream. It had to be.

But then I heard it again.

'Alfie . . .'

THE
PHANTOM
THIEF

Also available by Pete Johnson, and
published by Corgi Yearling Books:

THE GHOST DOG
*Winner of the 1997 Young
Telegraph / Fully Booked Award
Winner of the 1997 Stockton Children's
Book of the Year Award*

MY FRIEND'S A WEREWOLF
EYES OF THE ALIEN

THE
PHANTOM
THIEF

Pete Johnson

Illustrated by Peter Dennis

CORGI YEARLING BOOKS

THE PHANTOM THIEF
A CORGI YEARLING BOOK : 0 440 86370 8

First publication in Great Britain

PRINTING HISTORY
Corgi Yearling edition published 1998
3 5 7 9 10 8 6 4

Set in 12.5/15.5pt Century Schoolbook.

Corgi Yearling Books are published by Transworld Publishers Ltd,
61–63 Uxbridge Road, Ealing, London W5 5SA,
in Australia by Transworld Publishers,
c/o Random House Australia Pty Ltd,
20 Alfred Street, Milsons Point, NSW 2061,
in New Zealand by Transworld Publishers,
c/o Random House New Zealand,
18 Poland Road, Glenfield, Auckland,
and in South Africa by Transworld Publishers,
c/o Random House (Pty) Ltd,
Endulini, 5a Jubilee Road, Parktown 2193.

Printed and bound in Great Britain by
Cox & Wyman Ltd, Reading, Berkshire.

This book is dedicated to:
Jan, Linda, Robin, Harry and Adam;
and Anne Everall.

CHAPTER ONE

I don't scare easily.

I wanted to tell you that first because, well, lately, something very strange has been happening to me.

And I've been scared out of my wits.

It started just the other day when I was sent to the padded cell.

Mr Crumble (we call him Crumbly) made me walk in front of him. He kept one hand on my shoulder all the way, as if he was afraid I'd try and escape. The padded cell was right at the end of the corridor.

I'd never been in there before. No-one from my class had. I was the first. It was a weeny little room: dark and cold. There were broken chairs stacked up at the back, an ancient blackboard, a window about the size of my thumbnail and a wooden desk and chair for the prisoner.

'You can sit down.' Crumbly spoke very quietly. And his lips never moved.

'Now you are here for some training in your own time.' That's what he calls detentions: training. He told us that anyone whose name appears in his black book – 'the naughty book' – three times will have extra training. Since September, five people from my class have got their names in the naughty book once. No-one has been in there twice. And only one name appears three times. Mine.

But he's always watching me: just waiting to pounce. You ask anyone.

Crumble handed me a piece of paper. I had to write I MUST BEHAVE PROPERLY IN CLASS on both sides. That didn't seem too bad until I saw it was graph paper with hundreds of micro lines. If I missed even one line out I would be back here for more training tomorrow.

Crumbly paced around the room while I

wrote. Every so often he would lean over my shoulder. I could hear him frowning. He's got a grey moustache which exactly matches his grey suit. And none of his suits fit him properly. They are far too baggy. I'm sure he buys them at jumble sales.

He said: 'I have to go but I shall return very shortly. On no account are you to leave this detention room. Do you understand, Alfred?' (Everyone else in the whole universe calls me Alfie).

When he says my name he pronounces every syllable. 'Al – f – red.' I can mimic his voice. Once I did an impression in the classroom. It sounded exactly like him. Everyone was in stitches until they spotted him in the doorway. He didn't say anything. But he knew I was taking him off.

The next day I told a joke in his lesson. Mrs

Macey, my teacher last year, always used to laugh at my jokes, but he made me stand on my chair and told the class to laugh at me. He was trying to make a show of me. Then he said he was tired of the way I kept turning round to see if I'd got a reaction. So now my place is right at the back. None of my mates sit anywhere near me now.

I should have been writing my lines. Instead I sat staring up at all the cobwebs. There was a little forest of them around the light. And it had turned very quiet. It was as if someone had turned the volume right down. Not a sound. I didn't like it. It was kind of eerie.

It seemed as if everyone else had gone. That I was the only person left in the school. I picked up my pen and started to write. I love making up stuff. I can write stories for hours. I had this idea. I started writing.

A spaceship has landed. And the aliens have

sent everyone to sleep, except me. The aliens had forgotten about me in here. But not for long, as they've got supersonic hearing. They can hear a crisp packet being opened from a hundred miles away.

And moments later they burst into the padded cell. Soon it's full of aliens. They all have short spikey haircuts (hedgehog haircuts we call them), goofy-looking noses, jug ears and cheeky grins. In other words, they look exactly like me.

'We've come to take you back,' they said. 'Your real home is actually in another dimension on another planet. You've been trapped down on Earth long enough. Come and join us and be happy for the rest of your life.' I didn't argue. But I decided I'd better leave Crumbly a note.

'Dear Mr Crumble, I am off to my real home up there in the sky, far away from you. If I don't see you again I'll remember the good times.

This will take me no time at all, as there weren't any.'

I stopped writing. I gazed down in horror at what I'd done. I'd filled up both sides of Crumbly's graph paper with my story. He'd go mad when he read it. What could I say? My pen took my hand hostage. I could never let him see it. I shivered. It was getting cold in here.

I'd have been freezing if I hadn't been wearing my new jacket. A black bomber jacket.

I chose it. It has orange lining which is the best lining you can get. Mum wanted to put my name in it. She had this horrible cotton label all ready. But that would have made me look a right mummy's boy. In the end I let her sew the label inside one of my pockets. No-one would ever see it there, but it kept her happy.

I drew my jacket around me. It was too cold to write. Perhaps that could be my excuse. My fingers had gone numb.

I practised making my fingers look stiff. Then I looked up and nearly jumped out of my skin.

There was someone else in the room

A boy who looked exactly like me.

CHAPTER TWO

I gaped at him in amazement. Had I conjured him up? Had he wandered out of my story?

Now I was being daft. But I hadn't heard the door open. I just looked up, and there he was. Still, sometimes when I'm thinking hard I don't hear things.

The boy didn't move any nearer to me. He just stood by the door looking bewildered, as if he couldn't quite believe he was there. He was wearing our hideous, green uniform. Strange I'd never seen him before.

'Hello,' I said at last. 'What do you want?'

He didn't answer. He just looked very puzzled. Finally I walked over to him. Up close he didn't look so much like me. He was quite a bit smaller. And his hair was much longer. It looked like a bush. And he didn't smile at all. He was very serious.

He must be new. He'd been sent here as a joke.

'Are you new?' I asked.

He opened his eyes wide. But he didn't answer. I wondered suddenly if he was an exchange student from France or Germany. A group came over in the summer. Maybe he was from another one? If so, it was a bit mean directing him in here. Were some boys sniggering outside? I couldn't hear anyone.

'Do you speak English?' I asked.

'Yes,' he said, slowly. 'And I am in Mrs Porter's class.'

'Mrs Porter,' I repeated. 'There's no teacher here called that, I'm afraid. Still, I'm always getting people's names wrong. Perhaps you mean Mrs Macey. She was my teacher last year.'

He shrugged helplessly.

'Don't worry about it,' I said. 'Actually, you're not supposed to be here at all. This is the detention room, the padded cell we call it. I was sent here by this really mean teacher . . .'

Suddenly he swayed forward as if he was going to faint. I darted towards him and pushed him on to my chair. For a moment he sat there with his head in his hands. I didn't know what to do. Should I get help?

Then he started muttering something. I couldn't make out what he was saying. I crouched down. He was shivering. His face was deathly pale.

I heard him say: 'Need help.'

'You need help?' I prompted.

He looked up. He had the same large blue eyes as me. He looked so unhappy I felt sorry for him. I wanted to help. He seized hold of my sleeve.

'In danger.' I made out those two words. But I couldn't hear any more. His teeth were chattering too much. I felt uneasy. There was something wrong here. Something bad.

A shudder ran through me.

I got up. 'I'm going to get someone.'

He struggled to speak.

'It's all right. I'll get Mrs Macey. She's good at first aid and things. I won't be long. OK?

He didn't answer, just sat there shivering.

'It's freezing in here, isn't it?' I said. Suddenly, impulsively, I handed him my jacket. 'Borrow this for a sec.'

He stared at me uncertainly. 'It's all right. It won't bite you. Bung it on . . . it's a good jacket, isn't it? There, that should stop you freezing to death . . . Oh yeah, what's your name?'

This time he answered at once: 'Alfred.'

That gave me a real start. 'But that's incredible. You've even got the same name as me. Only everyone calls me Alfie – perhaps they call you Alfie too?'

But somehow he looked more like an 'Alfred'.

Suddenly he sat bolt upright. 'Alfie,' he cried really urgently. I think he wanted me to stay. I hesitated. But then another shudder ran through me. I wanted someone else in on this.

'Don't worry, I'll be back before you know it. Take it easy.'

I opened the door carefully. If they gave trophies for lurking, Crumble would have a shelf full of them. He was always lying in wait in the darkest part of the corridor: ready to jump out at you. I looked both ways as if I was about to cross the road. All clear. I thought some boys might be hovering: the ones who'd lured Alfred into the padded cell. Surely he wouldn't have wandered in there on his own.

And who was he? Still, the main thing for me was to get him help.

I scuttled along the corridor. Crumble could pop up at any moment. I hovered outside the staffroom. Mrs Macey was usually in the staffroom at lunchtime as she was quite old, and walked with a limp. Sometimes she'd sit with her feet on another chair. Please let her be in there today.

I decided not to knock on the door just in case Crumble was in there. I'd just take a quick peek. The staffroom door creaked open. Now I could see. The staffroom was empty except for one person. He had his back to me. He was taking some books out of a cupboard. I recognized the ill-fitting suit instantly.

Then I did something stupid: I panicked and let go of the door. It slammed shut with a bang that made me jump a foot into the air.

I fled back down the corridor.

I ran fast – I came seventh in cross-country out of the whole school – but not fast enough.

'Alfred Drayton.'

The words hissed down the corridor after me.

CHAPTER THREE

Mr Crumble was pointing his finger at me. It was only a few centimetres away from my nose. There were yellow stains on the tips of his fingers. That's because he smokes so much.

'Who gave you permission to leave the detention room?'

He never raised his voice, even when he was really angry – like now.

Instead his voice was even softer, so it was hard to make out what he was saying.

'There's a boy in the padd . . . the detention room,' I began.

'What boy?'

'He's a new boy, and he's called . . .'

'There's no new boy here today.'

'Oh, OK then,' I stuttered. 'Well, I've never seen him before but he looks really ill. I came to get him some help.'

Mr Crumble screwed his eyes up and peered down at me beneath his bushy eyebrows. He often does that when I'm talking to him. Then he said something I couldn't catch – maybe I wasn't meant to? – and started marching down the corridor.

Crumble thought I was messing about. He thought there wouldn't be anyone in there. I was about to prove him wrong. Then he'd have to say I'd done a good deed. It might even turn out I'd saved Alfred's life. That would be great.

Crumble opened the door. At first all I could see was Crumble's back. Then I heard him give this loud sniff of annoyance. I peeped over his shoulder.

I couldn't believe what I saw – or rather didn't see.

For Alfred had vanished.

I was so shocked I forgot to breathe.

How could Alfred have left without me seeing – or hearing anything? I'd only been a few metres away up the corridor. Besides, I doubted if Alfred could have tottered to the door on his own never mind wander off somewhere.

So where was he? People don't just melt through walls. I stared hopelessly around me. Crumble was prowling about too. He snatched up my story about aliens: 'Are these your lines?'

'Yes. No. Well, in a way.' Then I remembered that rude letter I'd written at the end of the story: 'Actually, it's private. Very private.'

Crumble didn't answer. He just went on reading. His greasy skin shone under the light. I stood stock still. I didn't know what to do.

At last Crumble stopped reading: 'Well, what's happened to your sick boy?'

My face burned. 'I don't know.'

'It's a real mystery.'

'Yes.'

'Maybe this boy was an alien?'

I looked at him in amazement.

'And maybe this alien could change shape so he turned into a beetle and escaped under the door?'

Crumble does that sometimes: makes these really dry, sarcastic kind of jokes. So if you get an answer wrong in class he'll mutter, 'It'd be easier teaching fish to read.' He thinks he's funny. He's about as funny as a cup of cold sick.

'You have wasted my time and your time,' said Crumble.

'There really was someone here,' I said.

Crumble ignored this. 'So you will undertake extra training at home tonight. This time you have four sides of lines to complete.'

'But that's not fair,' I began.

'It's your own fault – you've brought it on yourself,' murmured Crumble. 'It seems to me you've been watching too much television,

with all this silliness about aliens and phantom boys.'

A phantom. Was that what Alfred had been? Yet, he hadn't been at all shadowy or misty. And my hand didn't go through him when I helped him on to a chair.

He'd looked as real and as solid as me.

Only a lot less healthy. Then I remembered something else: something terrible.

That ghost or whatever he was had stolen my jacket.

CHAPTER FOUR

It takes me exactly nineteen minutes to walk home from school. I've timed it.

Of course if I run I can do it in half that time. But I don't often run home these days.

Today it took me fifty-six minutes to get home. That was because I went for a walk. I needed to think about what had happened at lunchtime. But it didn't help. Afterwards I was as confused as ever.

People can't just disappear.

It didn't make any sense.

I threw my bag across the floor. I was fed up.

27

My mum appeared. 'At last. Where have you been?'

Centuries ago I used to tell my mum everything about my day. But not now.

'Just here and there,' I said.

'And Alfie, look at your shoes,' exclaimed Mum. 'Did you spend the whole day wading in the mud? Take them off at once, then come into the kitchen.'

I flung my shoes into the shoe-box, then went into the kitchen. Mum was sitting at the table. Her glasses were perched on top of a pile of papers. She teaches at the college in the town.

'Sit down, Alfie.' Something was wrong, I could tell. 'I've just had your teacher on the phone.' I swallowed hard. Crumble strikes again. 'He tells me you ran out of his detention.'

'I didn't run out.'

'You said you'd seen an alien.'

I shook my head, 'That man is such a liar.'

'He said that instead of writing your lines you wrote a story about an alien who looked like you. Then you pretended the alien had turned up and needed help.'

'No, no.'

'All right,' said Mum. 'Tell me your side of it.'

I hesitated. 'It's hard to explain.'

'Did you write a story instead of doing the lines, as you were told?'

'Well, yes.'

'And did you leave the detention room?'

'Yes . . . but . . . I had no choice.' Mum looked at me expectantly. 'This boy turned up.'

'In the detention room?'

I nodded. 'And he was pretty ill, so I went to get help. But when I came back with Crumble the boy had gone.'

'Who was he?'

'I don't know. I've never seen him before.'

Mum sighed.

'It's all right you sighing,' I said, 'it was a very eerie experience.'

'What was?' asked Rachel from the doorway.

'Nothing to do with you,' I muttered. Rachel's my sister and she used to be all right. She had an earring in her nose, stayed out late every night and was always rowing with Mum. Sometimes I'd wake up at night and hear them screaming at each other. It was excellent. But lately Rachel's changed. She goes on and on about her exams and what grades she's hoping to get. She works for hours in her room every night.

Worse still, she and Mum have become all pally, going off shopping, then sitting together on the couch giggling over what they've bought. It's disgusting to watch.

And while Rachel just used to ignore me, now she's always nagging me about something. It's like I've suddenly gained another parent. (Just to let you know, my dad left home shortly after I was born. He's now got another family in Dublin. I haven't seen him for years. He sends me good presents on my birthday, though.)

'You're not in trouble again, are you?' demanded Rachel.

'Alfie's school rang up,' explained Mum. 'He didn't do his detention.'

'Don't tell her,' I said. 'It's none of her business.'

But Rachel had already pulled up a chair. 'That's all you need, isn't it, Mum?' She turned to me. 'Mum's been on her feet all day and she's back in the college this evening. Surely you can at least try and behave at school?'

'Like you did, you mean? Mum was always having to go up to the school about you.'

'That's enough,' said Mum.

'You're just so ungrateful,' said Rachel. 'Mum went out specially last week with you to get you a new jacket and this is how you repay her.'

Mum was looking curiously at me now. 'Where is your jacket, Alfie? You weren't wearing it when you came in.'

I stared miserably back at her. 'I loaned it to someone.'

'Who?' demanded Mum.

'That boy in the detention room, actually.'

'No, Alfie,' cried Mum. 'This really won't do. When you were younger it might have been funny to make up all these stories – but not now.'

'You've lost it, haven't you?' taunted Rachel.

'No, I'll get it back.'

'You'd better,' said Mum. 'I'm not buying you another one; that's got to last you the entire year.'

'We're not made of money, you know,' hissed Rachel.

'Just shut your mouth,' I hissed back. I didn't want to stay in this house another second. I'd go round to Grandad's. I could tell him what had happened. And perhaps he could even explain it. I got up.

'Where are you going?'

'I'm going to Grandad's,' I said. 'I'll have my tea round there.'

'Sit down,' said Mum. 'Before you do anything else, you'll finish those lines for Mr Crumble.'

When I showed Mum the graph paper he'd given me she did say, 'Oh, they're such small lines,' and a look of sympathy crossed her face. But then she said, briskly, 'Still, the sooner you start the sooner you finish.' After which, another bombshell: 'Oh yes, Mr Crumble said they are still looking for pupils to help at the Open Evening tomorrow, so I volunteered you.'

'You did what?'

Mum started to laugh. 'Now don't look so horror-struck, it won't do you any harm . . . and besides, you were at the last Open Day.'

'Yes, but then I was playing in the football demonstration. This time I'll be showing parents round. Only gimps do that.'

'Honestly,' said Rachel, 'why do you have to make such a fuss about everything? And I don't suppose Alfie's brought the logs in for the fire like he's supposed to.'

'I haven't had a chance,' I snapped.

'It's all right, I'll do it,' she said.

'Oh, are you sure, dear?' asked Mum.

Rachel gave her martyr's smile. 'No problem at all, Mum.'

'Creep,' I muttered at her. 'And I'm not going to that poxy Open Evening tomorrow,' I muttered under my breath.

'Oh yes you are,' replied Mum. 'I know you won't let me down.'

* * *

It was after seven when I finally escaped to Grandad's. It was a windy, drizzly October evening. Mum made me wear my old grey coat. She had chosen it for me and she's got terrible taste. It's even got a hood. I can't stand hoods, they're so babyish. I'd rather take a hat with me.

I took a short-cut to Grandad's down the alleyway. Mum doesn't like me going this way as there are no street lights. But tonight I was in a hurry.

Thick bushes crouched on either side of the pavement. Their leaves rustled in the wind. Suddenly I stopped. I had the strangest feeling someone was following me. It wasn't anything I'd heard. I just sensed it. I turned round. The darkness was full of shadows. Did one of those shadows move?

I began to walk faster. Was the person behind me walking faster too? A pile of dead

leaves flew up into the air. They made a strange, whooshing noise. It sounded eerie. I should have looked round again. But I was too scared at what I might see.

Instead, I shouted down the alley, 'Oh, there you are, at last.'

And I ran all the way to Grandad's, my breathing hissing in my ears. Then I tried to laugh at myself. But to be honest, I still felt shaken up.

Grandad's house stands back from the road behind a large hedge. He lives there with Molly, his dog. I rang on the doorbell. Usually Molly would be barking and sniffing at the door and I'd be telling her not to worry, it was only me.

But today, the house was horribly silent. And the only sound was Grandad undoing the chain and opening the door.

'Well, if it isn't young Alfie,' he said. My grandad is both young and ancient. He's got a bald, shiny head ('My hair is very seldom,' he says: that's one of his little mildewed jokes) and wears glasses with ugly, black frames. He dresses old, too: grey v-necked pullovers, brown trousers, sports jacket, and when he goes out a flat cap. (I really like his cloth cap though. He lets me borrow it sometimes.)

But my grandad also wears trainers – he says normal shoes can't support his feet. And he can move really fast in his trainers. In fact, from a distance you wouldn't think he was old at all.

'How are you, Alfie?' he asked.

'Terrible – I'm in trouble with Mr Crumble about . . .'

'If I had a pound for every time you've said that I'd be sunning myself in the Bahamas,' interrupted Grandad. 'I suppose you're going to tell me about it.'

I grinned at him. 'That's right, and I want to ask your opinion about something important.'

'Come in. We're in the study.'

'How's Molly?'

'Ah, she doesn't know she's born, sitting around all day, being carried everywhere. I told her not to get used to this.'

Grandad gave a kind of chuckle. But I wasn't fooled.

Molly's been Grandad's dog for nearly six years. After Nan died Grandad hardly went out. Mum thought a dog would help him get out again. I went with Grandad to the kennels where he first saw Molly. A black labrador.

She came right up to the edge of the dog cage. I knew she wanted us to take her: 'Now, that's a dangerous dog,' said Grandad, 'because if you let her, she'll break your heart.'

She settled in at Grandad's right away. And both Grandad and I would take her for long walks. It was just perfect until recently a bone in Molly's back became loose. The vet said it was too dangerous to remove it. And poor old Molly's back legs became paralysed.

The vet said it might be easier for Grandad if Molly was put down. And even my mum thought it would be too much for Grandad lifting Molly about everywhere.

But Grandad just said, 'She can use two legs, can't she – and that's as many as me.' Then this girl, Sarah, who lives next door to Grandad saw a photograph of a dog in a special dog trolley. It was in an American magazine. And Grandad sent away for one for Molly. He filled in this great long form giving all of

Molly's measurements. Now he was waiting for the trolley to arrive.

Molly was lying in her basket. Grandad had put it by the fire as that was her favourite spot. When she saw me she barked and thumped her tail. Usually I crouch beside Molly and sit stroking her for hours. I can hear her whimpering under her breath and I tell her not to worry; she'll be back on her feet again soon. But Molly just gives me this look, as if to say I've heard that before.

But today there was someone else stroking her: Sarah. She goes to my school. She's in my class, in fact. But I never speak to her. No-one does. Because she's dead weird. She hasn't got any friends – except for Grandad. She only moved next door to Grandad a few months ago. But she's got well-in with him and Molly already. She's always round their house now. It really annoys me.

Grandad brought in a jug of orange juice and a large plateful of biscuits. He told us to tuck in. In the past Molly would get up on her hind legs to beg for food. Today she just stared mournfully at us. I ended up giving her practically all of my biscuits.

'Look at that dog, she's getting thoroughly spoilt,' said Grandad. Then he asked me what I wanted to talk to him about. He didn't seem to realize that a stranger was there. I hesitated.

'Do you want me to go?' asked Sarah, staring at the carpet.

I did, very much. But I didn't think I could say that out loud. Then Grandad said, 'Well, young Alfie's in trouble again with Mr Crumble.'

'Oh, I know all about that,' she said, dismissively.

Stung by her tone I said, 'I don't think you do, actually.' But I wasn't going to say any more about what had happened with Crumble. That was personal. Instead, I said, 'Anyway, it's not exactly about that: Grandad, do you believe in things like ghosts?'

'Not at all,' said Grandad, so confidently I was quite surprised.

'But lots of people see them,' I said.

'Ah, but then imagination is a mighty powerful thing,' said Grandad. 'But that's all they are: a trick of the mind.'

I looked at him doubtfully.

'Listen, Alfie, if I said I saw little green ghosts outside the old church, within hours lots of other people would say they had seen them too. And they would think they had. But only in their minds.'

'So no ghost really exists?'

'Absolutely not,' said Grandad. 'There's a perfectly rational explanation for every ghost story.' Grandad was so firm about this I didn't know what to say next.

Then Molly started to bark and look at the door. 'Want to go out, do you girl?' asked Grandad. 'Off we go, then.' He put the special harness around Molly and picked her up. 'You two can finish off the biscuits while we're gone . . . but save one of the chocolate ones for me, or there'll be trouble.' Molly barked again. 'All right, girl, I'm going as fast as I can.'

After Grandad left the only sound was the fire crackling and hissing and Grandad's clock ticking away. I began to think about what Grandad had said.

When I thought I was being followed – well that could have been a trick of the mind, I suppose. But what about the boy in the padded cell? I couldn't just have imagined him. And what about my jacket. Where on earth had that gone?

'I believe in ghosts,' said Sarah, suddenly.

I looked up, shocked. I'd sat in this room with Sarah a number of times but we'd never said anything to each other, except a muttered 'hello'.

'Oh, do you?'

'And you've just seen a ghost, haven't you?'

I gazed at her, stunned. 'Why do you say that?'

She gave a strange kind of smile. 'But I'm right, aren't I?'

CHAPTER FIVE

'Yes, all right,' I said, 'I have seen a ghost. I saw it today, actually.'

There was definitely a flicker of envy in Sarah's eyes now. 'Where did you see it?' she demanded.

'In the padded cell.'

'The what?'

'The detention room.'

'Actually, padded cells don't have any furniture in them so you shouldn't really call it . . .'

'Do you want me to carry on with my story or not?'

Sarah looked huffy. 'Go on then.'

'This boy came in, about my age, looked a little bit like me. And he was pretty ill. Well if he was dead, I suppose he was very ill indeed.'

Not even the tiniest smile from Sarah.

'How do you know he was a ghost?' she asked.

'By the way he just disappeared. I went up the corridor to get help and when I got back he'd gone . . . vanished.'

'And he hadn't climbed out of the window?'

'An ant could just about climb out of that window. Nothing any bigger.'

'And there was no other way of escape?'

'No.'

'Not a trap door, or anything.'

'Oh yes, there was, actually. Dirty great thing. I popped down it myself.'

'There's no need to be sarky.'

'But what a stupid question.'

'I must explore every possibility,' she said.

'And you've got to remember that I know far more about ghosts than you. I've read more than fifty books about them.'

'But I've seen one.'

'You *think* you've seen one,' she corrected. 'Now tell me again what happened and don't miss out a single detail – then I'll let you know if you've seen a real ghost or not.'

At that point I nearly walked out. I nearly went out and joined Grandad and Molly in the garden. Talk about big-headed. No wonder no-one liked her.

But I didn't want to keep this story to myself any more. It was actually a relief to tell someone, even if it was the Smurf. That's what everyone in my class calls Sarah, because she's very small . . . and very annoying.

All the time I was talking, Sarah sat staring into the fire. She didn't look at me once until I'd finished.

'I've heard you make up stories,' she said.

'Have you?'

'Is this one of them?'

'You're the great ghost detective. You tell me.'

'Despite everything, I believe you,' she said, finally. 'I think you've seen a true ghost.'

A shiver ran through me.

'It's a well-known fact,' went on Sarah, 'that ghosts often haunt a place where something happened to them. Usually something bad.'

'Maybe Crumble murdered him in there?'

She sighed. 'Now you're just being silly again.'

'No more silly than you and your trap door.'

She ignored this. 'I expect the boy died in that room of some terrible disease. Now he keeps returning to the room. He can't help himself. I think we should go back there and wait for him.'

I looked up. 'We?'

'Yes, you'll need me as a witness. I can prove what you say – and show you're not going round the bend.'

'Well, thanks . . . but we can't just wander into the padded cell and say we're waiting for a ghost. Teachers would never allow it.'

46

She shook her head impatiently. 'Tomorrow night is the ideal time.'

'Tomorrow night?'

'Yes, during the parents' evening. When everyone is in the hall we can slip away to the detention room and watch for your ghost.'

That was such a good idea I was ashamed I hadn't thought of it.

'I've volunteered to help tomorrow,' she said, 'although I'm quite certain you haven't.'

'Well, that's where you're wrong,' I replied, enjoying the look of surprise on her face. 'Me, I never miss a good parents' evening.'

Before she could reply, Grandad and Molly had returned. I sat there, planning it all out. I certainly would ghost-watch in the padded cell tomorrow night. And I'd have someone with me as a witness, too.

Only it wouldn't be the Smurf.

CHAPTER SIX

It seemed strange walking back to school in the evening in my school uniform.

I arrived just as Mrs Macey was giving out our name tags. I was glad Mrs Macey was in charge tonight, not Mr Crumble. She was all right.

She was telling us what to do. But she kept fiddling with her buttons. Teachers always get nervous on parents' evenings.

She said we had to go up to each adult we saw and ask, very politely, if they would like to be escorted into the hall. Then we had to show them to a seat.

'Then can we put our hand out for a tip?' I asked.

'Just you dare,' said Mrs Macey. But she was laughing. You can have a joke with her. Practically everyone else smiled, except the Smurf, of course.

Sarah is skinny, and a bit spotty. She's got long, mousy hair, starey, green eyes, and she wears merit badges all down her blazer. You get merit badges for good work. I got some when I was in Mrs Macey's class. But I wear them on the inside of my blazer. You can wear them on the outside when you're about five. But not now. It just gives you a really bad image.

No wonder the other girls were giving Sarah dirty looks. I was glad I wasn't going to watch for the ghost with her. I looked around for

Michael. He was my best mate. Well, he still is. It's just I've hardly seen him since Crumble moved me to the back of the class.

He'll wait for that ghost with me all right. But there wasn't time to ask him as parents were already swarming about. This man with a face like a horse peered hopefully at me. 'Perhaps this young man can tell me where to go?' he said.

I didn't dare answer that one.

The next half hour was really busy. I amused myself by talking to the parents in different accents: Irish, Scottish, Brummy, and I even tried out an Italian one, although I don't think that was one of my biggest successes as the parents kept giving me odd looks. I have a feeling they won't be sending their children here.

Then I spotted Michael on his own. There was no time to mess about so I got straight into the subject.

'Hiya, Mike, do you believe in ghosts?'

'Not much. Why? Don't tell me, you've seen one.'

'As it happens, I have. And it's in this school, just upstairs in the padded cell.'

'In detention, is he?' said Michael grinning.

'No, he's . . . well, ghosts don't do a lot, do they? But he's up there, haunting away.'

'Oh, really,'

'No, listen, I've seen him . . .' I started to explain.

'Wind up, wind up,' interrupted Michael.

'No, it's not. I'm sure he's there and I just want a witness to come and see.'

He started backing away. 'No, sorry,' said Michael. 'I can't.'

'Why?'

'My mum and dad have promised me a new mountain bike for my birthday next week if I stay out of trouble.'

'Is that why you've hardly spoken to me lately?'

'No, of course not – it's just you're always in trouble with Crumble . . .'

'That's not my fault.'

'I know. But I've got other mates too.'

'And I hope you'll be very happy with them – and your new mountain bike.'

'Don't be like that,' said Michael. 'There isn't really a ghost upstairs, is there?'

'You'll never know now, will you?' I said and walked away.

I didn't care if I never spoke to him again.

Then I spotted Sarah. She was standing in the doorway with two other girls from my form. Most of the parents were in the hall now. They were waiting for any late-comers.

Mrs Macey rushed up. 'All right girls, and you, Alfie, . . . I think everyone's arrived, so you can come into the hall now. Sit quietly on the mats at the back.' She sped off again.

The two girls linked arms. They acted as if Sarah wasn't there, although I heard them mutter 'the Smurf' and then giggle. Sarah didn't react at all. Her face was a mask. Then she came over to me.

'I've just got to get something,' she said. 'Meet you at the top of the stairs . . .' she spoke out of the side of her mouth as if she was in a spy film.

'Yes, all right.' I supposed Sarah was better than no-one. Just.

And then she hissed after me: 'And don't let anyone see you.'

I just gritted my teeth in reply. Actually, the hall doors were closed so it was quite easy to sneak upstairs. I hovered around. All the classroom doors were open and inviting, while the walls were top-heavy with pictures. Only one door was firmly closed. No-one would be taken to the padded cell tonight. It was out of bounds for all visitors.

'Hello.'

I swung round. Sarah was beside me. She was carrying a large bag.

'Off on your holidays after this, are you?' I asked.

'I've brought our equipment,' she said.

'What equipment?'

'Oh, you'll see. Now hurry up, we haven't got a moment to lose.'

We half-ran down the corridor. The door to the padded cell loomed in front of us. I felt just a bit apprehensive.

'Do you think we should knock first in case the ghost's waiting for us?'

'Stop being silly and open the door,' said Sarah.

The door creaked open. Funny how I didn't remember it creaking in the day. I stared around me. I hate the way rooms grow in the dark. They stretch out for ever at night. Even midget rooms like this one.

I grabbed for the light switch. The room was lit up for one half second, then there was a pinging noise and thick darkness again.

'Bulb's gone,' said Sarah.

'Oh thanks for telling me. I'd never have guessed.'

Now, light bulbs explode all the time. The one on our landing went a couple of nights ago. That's the one my mum hates changing. So I did it for her.

Yet there seemed something ominous about it happening the moment we stepped in here. I started whistling under my breath. Soon my eyes would get used to the darkness. For now the room was full of dark shapes. Even Sarah was little more than a shadow.

I wished there was some kind of light in here. And then there was.

Sarah was waving a torch about. A pale, yellow light prowled restlessly around the room. It couldn't seem to settle. Little corners of the room were caught in its glare, just for a moment, before the light leapt on again. But there was nothing – or no-one here – I could see that. I should have begun to relax. But instead, my feeling of uneasiness grew.

Something wasn't right here. I knew it.

Finally I sat down at the prisoner's desk.

'Was that where you were sitting when you saw the ghost?'

Sarah's torch beamed in on me as I answered, 'That's right, this is the very spot.'

She sat down opposite me in the teacher's chair. Then out of her bag she produced a tape-recorder.

'What's that for? Going to interview the ghost, are you?'

'Maybe. Imagine if we got your ghost talking on tape.'

'He's not my ghost,' I muttered. 'I just happened to see him – and he's pinched my jacket. That's the first thing I'll ask him about.'

'I doubt he's actually stolen it,' said Sarah. 'Ghosts often move things about but they rarely keep them. Now, I've also brought some binoculars.'

'Sarah, we're in a weeny little room, not a field.'

'I know that,' said Sarah. 'But still, they could be useful if I want to get a closer look.'

'Don't tell me you've got a camera in there as well.'

'No point. Ghosts haven't got any reflection, have they?'

'How do you know that?'

'Oh it's a well-known fact. Ghosts can never be seen in mirrors so they can't be photographed either. I'll do my first report now.'

'But nothing's happened yet.'

'I know, but I just want to write up a few details.'

Then the only sound was her pen scratching over the page. She seemed to think this was some kind of adventure. I wished I felt the same way. But I didn't. I had the strangest feeling we shouldn't really be in here.

Sarah looked up. 'And you first saw the ghost

in the doorway, is that right?'

'Yes, I just looked up and there he was.'

In a moment would I look up and see him again? Would he come in here looking pale and ill, muttering about how he needed help again? I'd hate to be a ghost: just living the same piece of time over and over again. Could he never break free?

I sniffed. The room smelt old and musty. And then I heard something, a kind of rustling noise as if someone was folding up a newspaper. I looked up sharply. Sarah was still writing; one hand holding her torch. She obviously hadn't heard anything.

But then she called across to me. 'It's just the wind.'

'What is?'

'The noise that made you jump a moment ago; it's only the wind outside.'

'I know,' I said quickly.

'I think it's going to rain soon.'

'How fascinating.'

Sarah put her pen down, then I heard her whisper, 'Alfred.'

'My name's Alfie.'

'I'm not talking to you.'

'What?'

'I'm calling to Alfred. I can't wait any longer. I want to see him, Alfred . . . Alfred.'

A shudder ran through me. 'No, don't do that . . . don't call him up like that.'

'Why?'

'I don't know, exactly. I just don't think you should, because . . .' and then the breath caught in my throat. For I saw something move. Over in the corner of the room just by the blackboard there was a shape, a shadow. I wasn't exactly sure. But something was there. Was it him, Alfred, hiding in the shadows?

'What's wrong?' called Sarah. There was fear in her voice too.

'Over by the blackboard,' I cried. 'I saw something.'

'Is it Alfred?'

'I don't know.'

All at once Sarah was up and shining her torch about. I don't know why, but I felt she shouldn't.

'No, don't go over there . . . don't disturb it. I don't think it wants to be seen,' I whispered, frantically.

But Sarah was already over by the blackboard. 'There's nothing here,' she began. Then suddenly she let out this sharp cry and the torch just flew out of her hand. We were in darkness again.

'I hate you!' she yelled.

'Me, why?' I spluttered.

She didn't answer. Instead, she stumbled past and ran out of the door. I heard her feet padding furiously down the corridor. She sounded as if she was being chased by some great monster.

I started to breath in gulps. I didn't understand this. I staggered to my feet. I picked up her torch and waved it towards the blackboard.

And then I saw there was writing on the blackboard. Four words had been put down by some invisible hand. The words screamed out of the darkness at me.

YOU ARE IN DANGER.

CHAPTER SEVEN

YOU ARE IN DANGER. Where had those words come from? I didn't know. I just knew I had to get out of here. Somehow I managed to bundle up all Sarah's equipment first. I kept flicking the torch around me; its light seemed to keep whatever was in this room at bay.

Then I tore down the corridor. Where had Sarah gone? Had she run home? I had to talk to her. I wanted her to know that it wasn't me who had written that message. For that's what she'd assumed.

But also, I couldn't keep tonight locked away in my own head. I had to talk about this with someone – even if it was only the Smurf.

As I passed the hall I could hear clapping. But the parents' evening seemed far away from me. I had far more important things to think about now.

Outside, that musty smell from the padded cell still seemed to hang about me. I couldn't shake it off. I walked quickly, then froze. Sitting in the bus shelter across the road was Sarah. She had her head in her hands. She looked really miserable as if she'd just heard some terrible news. I crossed the road.

She never even noticed me. She didn't look up until I said her name.

'You forgot your bag,' I said.

She didn't answer, just glared fiercely at me. I put the bag down beside her.

'Why did you run off like that?' I demanded.

She turned away. I thought she wasn't going to answer. I hate it when people sulk. My sister sulks. But then she hissed, 'You think you're so funny, don't you? Well, go on, tell all your friends you got me to believe your stupid story. You made a fool of the Smurf, all right.' She was breathing really fast when she spoke. She

made me feel guilty – even though I hadn't done anything.

'Sarah, I didn't write that message,' I said, in this very reasonable voice: the one I use when I think my mum's about to have a go at me. 'I promise you, I didn't do it. I mean, didn't you see how scared I was?' That made her look at me. She didn't say a word. But she moved up along the seat. I sat down beside her. 'Do you believe me?' I asked.

She considered. 'Maybe you wrote it subconsciously?'

'I hope not, because that would mean I was going a bit loony. And I don't think I am . . . Grandad says there's a rational explanation for everything. So in this case someone must have put that message up there as a joke.'

'Who?'

'I don't know. Someone with nothing better to do who wanted to scare the next person in the padded cell.'

'But no-one ever does lessons in there,' said Sarah. 'And I'm pretty certain the last person to have detention in there was you. It just doesn't make sense – unless . . .'

'Unless what?'

'Unless that ghost wrote it as a kind of warning to you, or me. Probably you.'

'Thanks.'

'Perhaps that ghost can see into the future?'

'If he can, I wish he'd tell me how Man United are going to do on Saturday.'

'Oh, be serious,' said Sarah.

'Yeah, but come on, it's not much of a message, is it? If he'd written "You will die if you eat school dinners tomorrow", then at least I'd know what to do. But his message is so vague, it's useless.'

'Maybe he writes that message every evening,' said Sarah.

'You mean each night this ghost wanders

into the padded cell, writes "You are in danger" on the blackboard, then spooks off until the next night, when he writes the same thing all over again.'

'It's the most likely explanation,' said Sarah.

'Well, all I can say is that ghost wants to get himself a life . . . that's a joke, by the way.'

'I know.'

'And would it have killed you to smile?'

'Oh, I hardly ever smile,' said Sarah. She got up. 'We haven't finished our investigation, have we? We should really go back and see if this ghost materializes – that's the proper word for ghostly appearances – and ask him about the message.'

'Yeah, all right.' But I didn't move. I really didn't want to go back to that room again. Not now. I studied my watch.

'The meeting will be over now, so parents will be all over the place – and teachers. It'll be hard to sneak into the padded cell now. There's bound to be someone who spots us.'

'That's true.' Was there a note of relief in Sarah's voice?

'To be honest,' – I gave this strange kind of laugh – 'I wonder if that ghost isn't best left alone . . .'

'What do you mean?'

I hesitated. 'Well, it's hard to explain, but every time I see him I get the feeling that, well, something's wrong – or about to go wrong.' I stopped. Sarah was staring intently at me. 'Stop looking at me in that tone of voice,' I said. 'And listen, if you do want to go back there, I will. After all, two's safer than one.'

'No, you're right,' began Sarah. 'It's too late to go back now.' She picked up her bag.

'Shame you never got to tape him, though.'

'Shame you never got your jacket back,' said Sarah. 'Still, I expect it will turn up. He'll have put it somewhere you haven't thought of yet.' Then she added in a low whisper, as if he might be listening, 'Some ghosts enjoy causing trouble and, yes, those ones are probably best left undisturbed.'

But next morning I returned to the padded cell. Daylight made me brave – and angry. How dare that ghost write such a pathetic message. I was going to march in there and rub out 'You are in danger'. That would show him.

My chance came just before school had properly started. I was helping Mrs Macey pack up after the Open Evening. She wanted to know where I'd disappeared to last night. I told her

Sarah hadn't been feeling very well and so I'd taken her home.

'That was very kind of you,' said Mrs Macey in a suspicious voice. But she didn't say anything else. She was too busy.

Then the phone rang in the staffroom. And she disappeared. While I shot down the corridor to the padded cell. I opened the door. The room had shrunk again to its normal, poky size. I went over to the blackboard. I had my hankie all ready. But there was no need.

The message had gone.

But who had rubbed it out?

No-one would have been in here yet. My heart started to thump.

There was something weird going on here. Even in the daytime.

I ran outside. I never wanted to go into that room again.

At breaktime I told Sarah what I'd done. Her

eyes opened wide when I told her the message had vanished.

'But that's good,' I said. 'It means I'm not in danger any more. It's all over.'

I kept telling myself that.

I certainly never expected to see that ghost again.

CHAPTER EIGHT

After school I took off on my bike. I like just cycling around. It's never boring. There's always something new to see. Besides, cycling helps me think. I thought about that ghost in the padded cell. Would it be writing 'You are in danger' on the blackboard again tonight? And would it rub the message off before daylight?

I'd never know because I wasn't going back to that room, ever.

When I returned Grandad's car was parked

in the drive. Grandad never called around at this time. Something must have happened.

Was Molly all right?

Grandad opened the door. He looked as if he'd been up all night. He looked terrible.

'Grandad . . . ?' But I didn't dare ask him about Molly. I was too scared of what he'd tell me.

'We've been waiting for you, young Alfie,' he said.

'Me, why?'

'We need your help,' replied Grandad, mysteriously.

I followed him into the kitchen. Mum was there. And Sarah. I started when I saw her. But my eyes were already searching for Molly. Grandad never went anywhere without her.

Then to my great relief I saw Molly. She was sitting in what looked like a small box on wheels. 'Is that the dog-cart?' I asked.

'That's right,' said Grandad. 'Arrived first

thing this morning.' He started explaining how it worked. The wheels took the place of her back legs. But her front legs were free to move around, although there was a little belt around her tummy so she couldn't fall out.

'But it's excellent,' I said. 'I bet Molly loves it, doesn't she?'

'I'm sure she will love it,' replied Grandad cautiously. 'But she's still getting used to it at the moment.'

'So how far has she gone in it?' I asked.

'Not very far,' admitted Grandad. 'In fact, she hasn't gone anywhere, yet. But it's not for want of trying.'

'Grandad's worn himself out,' began Mum. 'I thought that dog-cart was supposed to make life easier for you.'

Grandad brushed this comment away with a wave of his hand. 'This dog-cart takes a bit of understanding. I mean, we don't just sit on a bike and ride off, do we? Anyway we need all hands on deck for this one. I've had a go and so has Sarah here, but as you're the one who taught Molly all her tricks . . .'

'Yeah, I'll have a go. Of course I will,' I said. And it was true; I was the one who'd taught Molly to beg, jump for a tit-bit, get her lead, and to turn door handles. Molly could get into every room in Grandad's house before she became ill.

'Don't worry, leave it to me – the master dog-trainer,' I said.

I pushed Molly out into the back garden. Then I crouched down and started whispering to her. I always do that before I teach her a new trick. 'Molly, you've got wheels,' I said, 'and those wheels will take you where you want. You can go anywhere in the world again. Just trust me, all right?'

Molly sat there looking at me out of one eye. She does that when she doesn't want to do something. She thinks if she can't see you very clearly you can't see her either.

And she didn't move an inch. Grandad and Sarah crouched down beside me and started talking to her again. Then we'd take it in turns to tug at the dog-cart with the lead which was attached to it.

But still Molly wouldn't budge. Until finally she slumped forward and put her head in her paws. She couldn't see us at all now. And that was just how she wanted it.

'Ah well, she'll get it eventually. It's still early days,' said Grandad. But his face was lined with anxiety.

Mum came out. 'I've cooked you a meal, Dad,' she said.

'I couldn't eat a thing,' he replied.

'Now you won't be any use to Molly if you don't eat. So come inside and eat it up while it's still hot . . . the children will keep an eye on Molly.'

'I don't know,' grumbled Grandad. 'The day you retire everyone starts treating you just like a kid again.' But he followed Mum inside.

'Molly,' I whispered urgently.

Not even her ears twitched.

'It's no good,' I said.

And then Molly started to whimper to herself. She was upset and confused. Sarah immediately put her arm around Molly. 'Don't you worry. We won't make you do anything you don't want to do . . . She looks tired,' she continued. 'Maybe we should give her a break, let her go to sleep for a while?'

'No,' I replied firmly. Molly was sleeping more and more these days. She was acting as if she was a very old dog. That worried me. 'We'll push her around the garden.'

Molly didn't seem to mind this at all. We went right to the top of the garden. When we passed the old shed Molly got excited.

'She remembers,' I said. 'In the summer I'd be in this shed a lot. I took it over after Mum got a new one. And I kept dog-chocs in there, didn't I, Molly?'

Molly was staring intently at me now with her melting, brown eyes.

'Come on then, let's see if there are any chocs left for you.'

I helped Molly inside and discovered two dog biscuits which she immediately wolfed down. Sarah hovered outside.

'I'd better go,' she said.

'You don't have to. Come in.'

Sarah stepped inside, looking all around her as if she was stepping into a mysterious cave, not a tatty old shed.

'No-one, apart from Molly, has ever been inside here. This is my private place.'

'I like it,' said Sarah.

'Do you? Well I'll give you a quick tour. On the floor there,' I pointed, 'you will spy some very ancient comics and cycling magazines and a few games, while above you on the first shelf are some of my favourite books. The other shelf has only one thing on it: my cycling trophy. It's the only trophy I've ever won. I won it two years ago, so it's practically an antique now. But I'm hoping to have a twin for that trophy in a couple of weeks. I'm in this year's Junior Cycling Race.'

'Well, I hope you win.'

'So do I. Anyway, tour over, that's five pounds please.'

'A bargain,' said Sarah. 'I wish I had somewhere like this: somewhere to go, apart from my bedroom.'

'The only thing is,' I said, 'I'll have to get a heater in here. It's freezing . . .'

Suddenly Molly began to growl. Fierce growls which began deep in her throat.

'What is it, Molly?' I asked.

'She can probably hear the squirrels; they are often in our garden at night now,' said Sarah.

Molly's growling grew louder.

'It might be nothing,' I said. 'But Molly's a pretty good guard dog, you know. One night she started howling and wouldn't stop. Next morning Grandad discovered there'd been a burglary just down the road.'

'Shall I go and see then?' said Sarah.

'It's all right,' I said firmly. 'I'll go. You stay here with Molly.'

'Don't scare the squirrels, will you?' called Sarah after me. 'They're really such timid creatures you know.'

'It must be amazing knowing all about ghosts . . . and squirrels,' I muttered.

Outside the wind stung my cheeks. It had turned 'proper chilly' as Grandad would say. The wind sent the leaves scurrying across the grass. I was certain Molly had heard an animal in the garden. But I didn't think it was a squirrel.

Up at the top of our garden we get rats. They live next door in their compost heap. Then they creep over to our house at night. My mum's always complaining about them. But I like rats. They fascinate me.

I stood by our fence. I couldn't see a thing. But Molly was barking like crazy now. There must be something out here. I stared across at the garden. And that's when I saw something move. A shape. Only it was bigger than an animal. Much bigger.

Someone really was out here. A human. Was it Sarah? Had she wandered out of the shed to see what was going on? That would be just like her.

'Sarah,' I hissed.

The shape glided towards me. The face was shadowy and hard to see at first. It was the green I spotted. The green of my school uniform.

The ghost was here – in my back garden.

'What are you doing here?' I cried, my voice wobbling.

He didn't answer. He just kept oozing

towards me, his feet making no sound. Now I could see he was smiling. A terrible, hideous smile.

Then I heard him whisper my name. 'Alfie.' That made it even worse. I knew it was no accident he was in my garden. He had come looking for me. I should get away from him. But I couldn't move. I was rooted to the spot. It was as if he'd put me under some kind of spell.

I must get away. I knew I was in danger. 'Help.' But the word seemed to be trapped in my throat. 'Help,' I croaked again.

Out of nowhere came this loud bang. I jumped in the air. I thought it was a gun going off. Then something came charging towards me: a dark, furious shape. It ran right at me. I nearly fell over.

'What the . . . ?' I began. Then I started to laugh with relief and astonishment. 'Molly,' I cried. 'Did you hear me? Did you come out to

protect me?' I bent down beside her. Molly was panting and looking confused as if she couldn't quite believe what she'd done. For the ghost had gone, fading into the air like smoke. But my heart was still roaring inside my head.

Then I saw Sarah coming towards us. 'Isn't it wonderful!' she exclaimed. 'Molly was in the shed getting more and more worked up until she just leapt up, pushed open the shed door and flew outside. I wonder what made her do that?'

'It was me,' I said. 'Molly heard me calling for help.' I stood up.

For a second Sarah thought I was messing about. But then she realized I wasn't. Her voice tightened. 'Do you know what's out here, then?'

'Oh yes,' I said, grimly. 'And that's not such great news. It was that ghost, the one I saw in the padded cell.'

'What! So are you sure?' Suddenly she sounded frightened and anxious; Molly gave a low growl as if in sympathy.

'Of course I'm sure.' My voice rose. 'It was standing right in front of me.'

'But what's it doing here?'

'I was hoping you could tell me. You're the

one who's read fifty books about ghosts.' We were practically screaming at each other.

'Somehow that ghost's followed me home!' I cried. 'It even called me by name.'

'Oh no!' cried Sarah.

'What do you mean by that?'

'Nothing really, only . . . but no, that can't be true.'

I glared at her in mounting frustration. But there was no time to ask her anything else, as there were new voices in the garden.

'What are you shouting about?' demanded Mum, marching towards us. Grandad was with her.

But then Grandad spotted Molly. 'Here, girl,' he whispered. But I don't think he expected Molly to start moving towards him. But that is what she did. She didn't run or anything. Instead, she crept towards Grandad as if she was stalking a bird: very warily and slowly. But she was walking again with her new legs. It was just wonderful to see. Grandad was so chuffed he couldn't speak at first. Then he looked up at me. 'That's magic, that is,' he said. 'Well done, lad.'

'What did you do?' asked Mum.

I felt a right fraud. 'Oh, well, nothing really,

I got Molly to think I needed rescuing . . . and she forgot all about her fear.'

'Just magic,' repeated Grandad. 'There'll be no stopping her now, will there?' He rubbed Molly's head. 'I think we'll both be good for a few more years yet, eh girl?'

'You'd better be,' I said.

Mum invited Sarah to stay for tea. The four of us, and Molly, sat round the table – then Rachel came back from a friend's house.

Grandad and Molly did a special demonstration for Rachel. But Rachel just said, 'It's like she's moving in slow motion.' Rachel didn't understand at all.

Then Grandad invited Sarah and me round tomorrow for our tea. I never got a chance to ask Sarah any more about the ghost. I had a feeling she was avoiding me. But later that night she called.

'I'm sorry I wasn't much help tonight,' she

said. It was unusual for Sarah to apologize about anything. 'But I just want you to know I'm taking all my books on ghosts to bed with me. One of them must be able to explain how that ghost turned up in your garden tonight.'

'Earlier you started to tell me something.'

'Did I?' she said vaguely.

'You know you did.'

'Look, I'd rather not tell you any more until I've had a chance to do some more research.'

'Tell me now.'

'Well, I don't want to scare you.'

'Just spit it out.'

'All right. I think we might have been on the wrong track. I don't think that ghost is haunting the detention room – it's haunting you.'

'What!' I exclaimed.

'Now, I don't know for sure. But I think it's very strange you're the only one who ever sees it.'

'I don't want to keep seeing it. I'm quite happy for someone else to take a turn. Like you, for instance.'

'There's no need to be nasty. I'd be very interested in seeing that ghost. You know I would. But it never materializes for me . . . only to you.'

'So why is it haunting me?'

'That, I don't know . . . yet. But as soon as I work it out I'll give you a call.'

'How kind. Meanwhile this ghost could pop up at any time.'

'Yes, I suppose so.'

'Great – you've really cheered me up, haven't you? I'm sure I'll sleep better for knowing that. Thanks, Sarah.'

'You're the worst person ever. I don't know why I'm helping you.'

'Well, you haven't actually helped me,' I began.

At that Sarah rang off. I knew I'd been mean to her. It wasn't really her fault. I just had to take it out on someone. For I was becoming more and more confused – and scared. Something was going on here. Something bad. But I couldn't begin to understand it.

It took me ages to get to sleep. I'd jump awake thinking the ghost was in my room. Then I dreamt it had turned into a bat, swooping down on me out of the darkness. I even saw its fangs. I yelled and woke myself up.

What a relief. Except when I opened my eyes it was pitch dark. That really thick blackness, like a great fog. I hate waking up at this time. I tried to snuggle down into bed. I was just closing my eyes when I heard something.

Someone was calling me.

Years ago when I was in the bath one night this high, thin voice rose up out of the darkness calling, 'Alfie, Alfie.' I shook for the rest of the night. Later I discovered there was another, older Alfie who lived across the road from me. That voice was his mum calling him in to bed. I often heard her after that. But her voice still sounded strange and spooky. I was secretly very relieved when they moved away. And I never heard anyone else calling to me out of the darkness.

Until now.

It was a dream, the end of a dream. It had to be.

But then I heard it again.

'Alfie.'

It sounded nearer this time. If I opened my eyes would I see a figure in pale green uniform? Would he give me another of his terrible smiles?

What was he doing here? Why was he tormenting me like this? I should face up to him, tell him to leave me alone.

And in the daytime I could have done that. I'm not a total coward. But right then I was. I just buried my head under the covers whimpering slightly, like Molly. It was dark under there too. But it was a different kind of darkness. And it was very warm. I sank deeper and deeper into the warmth.

I stayed there until it was light. Then I peeped out. He'd gone. But I knew he'd be back. Sarah was right.

It wasn't the padded cell he was haunting: it was me.

CHAPTER NINE

Next day moved like a slug. I was dead tired but Crumble kept asking me questions in class. 'Glad you're still with us,' he said to me in his sarky way. But my mind kept drifting back to the ghost. The way he'd just suddenly appeared in my garden. That horrible smile.

Where was he now? Would I look up and see him staring in the window at me?

I didn't see him, but I had a horrible feeling he wasn't far away.

I watched out for Sarah. I needed to talk to

her. But she wasn't at school. That seemed a bit strange. She'd been healthy enough last night.

After school I was going round to Grandad's for my tea. But I called in at Sarah's house first. I wondered what my friends would say if they could see me: calling for the Smurf.

Her mum answered the door. She had steely grey hair and looked nearly as old as Grandad. She smiled welcomingly at me.

'I just wondered if Sarah was all right?' I said.

'She's much better now thank you . . . She had one of her heads,' she added, as if I knew all about it. 'You're Alfie, aren't you?'

'That's right.'

'Well, come in, come in.'

Sarah was sitting at this large, old table. She was writing in her notebook. She looked surprised to see me.

88

Her mum treated me like royalty. 'Now sit down on the sofa in the corner there, Alfie,' said Sarah's mum. 'That's the most comfortable chair in here. Is that all right for you?'

'It's fine.'

'And would you like a glass of orange and a biscuit, Alfie?'

'Not just now, thanks.'

'Are you sure? Well you're most welcome. We worry it's rather lonely for Sarah here all the time without even a brother or sister to talk to, just us old-timers. And we don't bite, you know. In fact, we're very friendly.'

Sarah sat there squirming. And after her mum had gone she said, 'I'm really sorry about that.'

'That's OK; all parents are embarrassing, it's compulsory. Sorry, I was a bit snidey last night.'

'You'd had a shock.'

'That's true – how are you feeling?'

'I haven't been ill,' said Sarah briskly. 'I've been doing some research for you.'

'Oh, thanks . . . by the way, you might want to put this in your notebook: it turned up again.'

Sarah was staring intently at me now.

'Where?'

'In the middle of the night it started calling my name out.'

'And did you see it?'

'No, it was too dark.' I didn't add that I was hidden under the covers at the time.

Sarah sucked her pen thoughtfully. 'I don't understand why this ghost should fix on you of all people.'

'Oh, thanks.'

'I've been thinking about it all day. I've got some theories.'

'Go on.'

'He might be trying to get a message to you.'

'Well, why doesn't he just say his piece and go.'

Sarah shook her head.

'Besides, what could a ghost possibly have to say to me.'

'All right,' said Sarah sharply. 'It's only a theory. I've got another one.'

'Amaze me.'

'You see, some ghosts are what they call mischievous. They like playing little tricks on people. I suppose it must be quite frustrating being a ghost.'

'My heart bleeds for them . . . and so you

reckon he likes stirring things up for me and giving me a scare?'

'I think so – although I expect Molly gave him a bit of a scare last night.'

'Yeah, she was brilliant, so I should be safe around Grandad's house tonight anyway.'

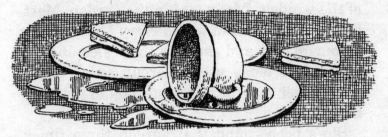

'Oh, I don't think the ghost will come anywhere near you while Molly's about. Animals are very psychic, you know.' She got up. 'There's something else about this haunting . . . a kind of missing piece of the jigsaw. Once I've worked that out I'll have cracked the case. So leave it to me – I'm really good at solving puzzles.'

'But you're really good at everything, aren't you, Sarah?'

Sarah did a blinky double-take. 'I don't have to help you, you know.'

Next door Grandad was waiting for us. 'Come into the kitchen,' he said. Then he pointed out

of the window. Molly was in the garden. Most afternoons Grandad would carry Molly to her favourite spot and she'd lie there sleeping for hours. But today was different; today Molly was on her feet (or paws) sniffing everything in the garden.

'She's been round that garden three times while I've been watching her,' said Grandad.

'She's catching up with all the smells she's missed,' I said.

'Actually,' said Sarah, 'she's reclaiming her territory; all dogs do it.'

'Took her out for a walk today,' said Grandad. 'We just went up to the top of the road and back, but I must have been gone an hour. We kept being stopped. It's true, you know, you speak to a lot more people when you've got a dog.'

'She'll be giving her pawprint for autographs soon. She's a star, like me,' I said. 'Incidentally, Grandad, this is not exactly a hint or anything, but I'm starving.'

'Tell me something I don't know,' replied Grandad. 'We can start taking the food into the living room, but I thought we'd better wait for our other guest.'

'What other guest?' I demanded.

'Oh didn't I mention it?' said Grandad. 'We're being joined by an old friend of mine, a lady-friend, actually.'

'A lady-friend,' I echoed contemptuously. I hope this didn't mean Grandad was going to spend the evening staring dreamily into the eyes of some old trout, like those couples on coffee adverts.

'She's just a very old friend,' said Grandad. 'I hadn't seen her for years, but she's here visiting, so I invited her round for tea – that's all.' But his neck had turned bright red and he half-ran into the living room.

'You are mean,' hissed Sarah.

'What?'

'Didn't you notice your grandad was all dressed up in his smart brown jacket.'

'I didn't, actually.'

'Well he obviously likes her, and why shouldn't he have a friend in his twilight years?'

'Because he's got me – and Molly – and even you, I suppose. And that's plenty.'

Grandad appeared out of the living room. 'Come on, you two, stop gassing. Put some food out.'

In the kitchen Grandad started piling these sandwiches on to a plate. The pile grew higher and higher until it looked like a skyscraper.

'Who is this woman who's coming round, Grandad?'

'She's called Mrs Porter.'

I considered. 'Mrs Porter. I've heard that name.'

Grandad shook his head. 'No, you wouldn't know her. You see . . .' At that moment the doorbell rang.

'Ah, that must be her,' said Grandad.

'Not necessarily,' I replied. 'It could be Father Christmas calling early.'

'I'll give you Father Christmas,' muttered Grandad.

A moment later I heard a woman's voice say, 'I'm not too early, am I?' and Grandad say, 'No, of course not.' They went into the living room. He introduced her to Sarah, while I hovered uncertainly in the doorway. I hate meeting people for the first time. Finally, I took a deep

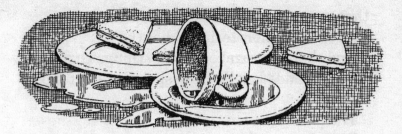

breath and joined them.

Mrs Porter had her back to me. She was talking to Sarah. But Grandad spotted me. 'And this is my illustrious grandson, Alfie.'

Mrs Porter turned round. A large woman in a green suit. She was smiling. Then she wasn't. And instead, she gave me this really funny look, as if I'd just dropped hot jam down her neck.

She let out this gasp, swayed a bit, then Grandad sprang forward and helped her on to the sofa. He knelt beside her, while Sarah opened a window.

'Oh dear,' cried Mrs Porter, 'I'm sorry about that.'

'Don't worry, you probably got too hot,' said Sarah. But I knew that wasn't what had happened.

I knew it was me.

One look at yours truly was enough to send

that woman spinning off into darkness.

I'd shocked her, terrified her.

And then I remembered something. That day in the padded cell, he'd spoken about Mrs Porter.

The ghost.

Was this something to do with him too? Had he somehow wormed his way in here? Was nowhere safe from him?

Mrs Porter smiled apologetically at Grandad. 'I thought I was going to pass out then.' Grandad told her not to worry; it was a humid evening. Sarah started fussing about with the cushions.

I didn't move. I felt oddly guilty. Then she sat up. She saw me. For a moment that look of terror returned. Her hand actually jerked.

After which she tried to recover herself. 'I'm sorry . . . It's . . .' She seemed to be searching for words. 'It's just uncanny,' she whispered, at last.

Then she tried smiling at me. And that made it even more eerie. Grandad was bewildered. He thought she was rambling. He said she needed a sugary drink. But Sarah kept looking across at me, her eyes nearly as wide as Mrs Porter's.

Propped up on her cushions Mrs Porter started to talk. 'You look exactly like an ex-pupil of mine.' She spoke very slowly, as if she'd just woken up from a heavy sleep. 'He was such a brilliant pupil. Yet he was also painfully shy, poor lad . . .'

'He's dead now, isn't he?' I interrupted.

'Yes, I'm afraid so.' Her voice fell away. 'It was very sudden. A dreadful shock.'

'And was he called Alfred?' asked Sarah.

'Why, yes, dear. Alfred Goddard. However did you know that?'

'Just a lucky guess,' murmured Sarah.

'And did he die at the school?' I asked suddenly.

Mrs Porter looked taken aback by the question. 'At school – why, no, he didn't.'

'But he looked a bit like young Alfie, here?' said Grandad.

'He's the spitting image of him,' said Mrs Porter.

'Oh no, he isn't,' I said. 'I'm much better looking for a start.'

'Listen to him,' said Grandad. 'You'd think he'd seen this boy. I'm afraid he was a bit before Alfie's time, wasn't he?'

'Oh yes, he must have died twenty . . . no, nearer thirty years ago.' She gave a funny little laugh. 'I must admit, when I first saw Alfie here, I thought he was a ghost.'

Grandad laughed too. 'First and last time you've ever been mistaken for a ghost, eh Alfie?'

I smiled grimly.

Then from outside came a loud, indignant bark from Molly. 'Poor old Molly's feeling all left out,' said Grandad. 'I must bring her in for you.' But Mrs Porter asked Grandad not to let Molly get too near as she was very nervous of dogs.

'She won't hurt you,' said Grandad.

'They all say that.' replied Mrs Porter. Grandad's smile slipped away. I had a feeling he wouldn't be inviting Mrs Porter round again for a while. Alfred wasn't mentioned any more. Although every so often I'd catch Mrs Porter giving me these 'looks' as if she couldn't believe I was real. I think she still found me a bit spooky.

Afterwards Sarah and I stood chatting outside her house.

'I don't know. First of all, you see a ghost. Now you're mistaken for one,' said Sarah lightly.

'Yeah, it's been quite a week,' I replied, equally lightly. 'I bet that Mrs Porter will dream about me tonight.'

'Poor woman,' said Sarah. 'I hadn't realized you looked so much like this Alfred.'

'I don't, really.'

'Are you sure?'

'I have met the geezer. And I'll probably see him again tonight: no doubt he'll have some more late-night entertainment for me.' The smile froze on my lips. 'I nearly asked Grandad if I could borrow Molly tonight, you know.'

'You should have done.'

'Nah. My mum would go mad for a start. She didn't like me keeping hamsters in my bedroom. She thinks pets should be kept outside – they're unhygienic, all that rubbish. So it'll just be me and the ghost again tonight. How long do you think he'll stick around?'

'I'm not sure,' said Sarah. 'Look, I am still investigating this case and I'm sure I'm going to make a breakthrough really soon.'

The following evening I'd just finished my tea when Sarah rang up. 'Did you see the ghost last night?'

'No, I was dead to everything. I didn't wake up once. So maybe he was calling to me but I never heard him – you were away from school again.'

'Was I? Well, I never knew that.'

'Hey, I'm the sarky one.'

'But listen to this,' said Sarah. 'I've cracked the case.'

'What.'

'Yes, I've worked it all out.'

'So tell me, tell me.'

'Well I'm not sure you're going to like it.'

'Why?'

'Look, I think it's best if I come round.'

'All right, sure – but why can't you tell me over the phone?'

But Sarah had already rung off.

CHAPTER TEN

I told Mum Sarah was coming round. Mum looked pleased. 'She's a nice girl, isn't she?'

'Not particularly,' I replied. 'But I've got to discuss something with her. We'll be in the old shed.'

Mum brought out a fan heater and a bean bag for Sarah to sit on.

I went back inside. I was getting impatient. Then I saw Sarah in our little porch. I saw her through the pebbled glass on the front door. I pulled open the door just as her hand touched the doorbell. She jumped back in surprise. I love doing that to people.

Inside the shed I switched on the heater. It whirred away. I was glad Mum had brought it. It was really cold in here tonight. Sarah sat on the bean bag. She was wearing a sports jumper and jeans. She dressed better out of school. She was also wearing these Kickers lookalikes. But they weren't real Kickers. I can always tell. I was sprawled out by the door. I made some silly comments – as I usually do – but my throat felt dry.

Sarah stared down at her notebook. 'I wanted to find out more about your ghost. Now we know his name was Alfred Goddard.' She sounded as if she were reading out her home-work in class. 'Mrs Porter said he died nearly thirty years ago. So I thought there must have been something in our local paper about him – and his accident. And they keep all the local

102

papers at the library, don't they?'

I gave her a 'get on with it' nod.

'Now I know the librarian, and she was very helpful. We went through all these old papers and discovered Mrs Porter was wrong. Alfred Goddard didn't die nearly thirty years ago. He died *exactly* thirty years ago.' Then with something of a flourish she unfolded a piece of paper from the back of her notebook. 'I made this copy for you.'

I stretched across and took the photocopy. There was a headline: 'TEN-YEAR-OLD BOY DIES IN CYCLING ACCIDENT' and a photograph. The picture was smudged but I recognized the boy all right.

'As soon as I saw the face I knew why Mrs Porter was so upset,' said Sarah.

'What do you mean?'

'He could be your double.'

'Sarah, if you want to live you'll stop saying that.'

'Why?'

'I should think that's obvious.'

'Not to me.'

'All right, for a start he's about as ugly as Quasimodo.'

'Don't be silly.'

'And look at his hair. It's like a mop. Turn him upside down and you can wipe the kitchen floor with that hair.'

'All right.'

'He's just a total geek. Something no-one's ever called me.'

'You're lucky,' said Sarah quietly. 'Look, calm down; his personality is obviously totally different to yours, except for one thing: you both love cycling. In fact, that was how he died, you know. He was out on his bike when he collided with this lorry.'

'I'm not really interested.'

'But you have to know one thing for your own safety.'

I looked across at her: 'What are you talking about?'

'Alfred Goddard died on October 29th 1967: that's thirty years ago next week.'

I shrugged my shoulders.

'But that's the day you're in the cycling race.'

That did give me a jolt. I'll admit that. But I quickly recovered. 'So what.'

'Well maybe it's nothing,' said Sarah, 'but it's a very strange coincidence, isn't it?' She leaned forward. 'I think it's best you pull out of the race.'

'You're joking.'

'Not at all.'

I shook my head in amazement. 'I don't believe you. I've been practising for this race for weeks. I've collected all the sponsorship money.'

'I know that,' said Sarah. 'But listen, there's something else I've got to tell you.'

'I can't wait.'

'I've been doing some reading about this, and what happens when you see a ghostly apparition who's your double – or time-twin, that's the proper term for it. So Alfred is your time-twin.'

'No, he's not,' I muttered through clenched teeth, 'because he's not my double.'

Sarah ignored this. 'Well usually the time-twin brings chaos with it. There was this story of a teacher who was sitting at her desk when all the pupils burst out laughing because they could see her time-twin out in the playground. The teacher ran up and down the playground but she never caught her double. And this kept happening until, in the end, the teacher got the sack. She – or rather her time-twin – was just too much trouble. But,' Sarah leaned forward, 'she was one of the lucky ones. Usually when people see their time-twin they meet their doom shortly afterwards.'

'You mean they snuff it?'

'Yes. And I'm not saying this to worry you. But if I didn't tell you and then something bad happened I'd feel dreadful.'

'I don't think I'd feel too good either. So I'm doomed, am I?'

'Well, you might be. Yes . . . sorry.'

I tried to laugh. But my breath caught somewhere in my throat. For a moment the only sound was the heater whirring away: it was a noisy heater, but totally useless. For the shed was still freezing cold.

I didn't want to stay here another second. And I didn't want to hear any more of Sarah's fanciful nonsense either.

I stumbled to my feet.

'What you're forgetting, Sarah, is that I don't think this ghost is my double. I bet there are hundreds of people who look more like me than him, probably hundreds of ghosts too.' Sarah stared up at me, surprised by my outburst. 'Anyway, if we stay here any longer we'll both be covered in frost. So shall we go?'

Now Sarah looked even more surprised.

'And I don't want this, thanks.' I thrust the photocopy back at her. She took the photograph from me, then gasped. It fell out of her hands.

I looked at her. 'What's going on?' I asked quietly.

Her voice was even lower. I could hardly hear her. 'I was just going to ask you to switch the heater off . . . it's boiling hot.'

A shudder ran through me. 'But it's like the Arctic in here.'

'No it isn't, Alfie,' whispered Sarah, urgently.

Suddenly she got to her feet. She walked over to me. She stood very still. Then she said softly: 'It even smells colder around you.'

'All right, all right,' I snapped. 'Don't make a big deal of it. I've just been standing in a draft.' I dashed over to where Sarah had been sitting. 'I'll soon warm up now.' I stood there, willing myself to get warmer.

Sarah didn't move at all. She looked like a figure in a wax museum. 'Feel any warmer?' she asked anxiously at last.

'Yeah, a bit,' I muttered. But I didn't. None of the heat was reaching me. It was as if there was an invisible wall of cold all around me. And nothing could get through it.

I couldn't fib any more. 'I can't get warm, Sarah.'

'Oh,' said Sarah, but it was more like a cry.

'I feel like someone's dropping ice down my back. Freezing cold ice.'

'Actually, ice can only be cold, otherwise . . .' The expression on my face made Sarah shut up.

'Well don't just stand there like a frozen robin,' I cried. 'Do something.'

'Yes, yes, of course. Just tell me what to do and I'll do it.'

'I don't know what to do – I don't know.' My voice was starting to shake all over the place. 'Sarah, what's happening to me?'

She took a deep breath. 'Well, don't panic or anything, but I think he's here. Your ghost.'

'Don't call him my ghost!' I practically screamed.

'Sorry, sorry. But it's him anyway.'

'Oh great – great. What's he doing this for anyway? What is he . . . ?' But I couldn't say any more. The words died on my lips. For my trophy had suddenly come to life. It was jumping about my shelf like a clockwork toy that had just been wound up. Then it shot right up into the air.

Sarah sprang back in horror as it whizzed around the shed. I pressed my feet hard on to the floor. I had the weirdest sensation that any second I might float off too. I swayed slightly, while unseen hands started tugging away at my magazines. The magazines twitched and shook and then they were flapping above our heads like giant bats.

Then I heard a strange, whimpering noise. That was me. I was scared out of my wits. Sarah grabbed hold of my sleeve. She didn't need to say a word.

We fled.

We ran – me skidding in my haste – into the house. We fell gasping into the kitchen.

'Alfie, have you got my hair-dryer?'

I looked up to see my sister staring accusingly at me. If she loses something she always goes, 'Alfie, have you got it?' She'll keep on asking me as well. Normally it really annoys me and I decide I will take something of hers just to get my own back. But tonight it was almost a relief; it seemed to bring everything back to normal.

'What would I want with your hair-dryer?'

'Well if I find it in your room,' said Rachel, 'I'm going to tell Mum.' She gave me one of her long looks. But she didn't ask why Sarah and I were out of breath. Perhaps she didn't even notice.

Then she flounced off.

I paced up and down. I was still shivering. But I was getting warmer – at last.

'I think he's gone,' I said.

'Good,' cried Sarah so firmly I couldn't help teasing her.

'I thought you were the one who wanted to see ghosts – it was one of your ambitions.'

'Not ones like him who just act silly.'

At once I was angry again. 'He's got no right to keep bothering me, has he? It's like he's stalking me.'

Sarah looked up. 'The Ghost Stalker – I suppose I ought to write this up while it's still fresh in my mind.'

'I don't think we'll ever forget what happened tonight.'

'That's true.' Sarah dug in her pocket for her notebook. It wasn't there. 'I must have left it in the shed. Oh, well, I can always pick it up another time.'

I nodded in agreement. But then I said, 'What are we saying? That's my shed. And no poxy ghost is keeping me out of there. I'll get it now.'

'Are you sure?'

'Yes,' I said as confidently as I could. I felt brave and scared, bits of each.

'Well, I'll come with you,' said Sarah.

'OK, let's do it fast then,' I said. 'I think it's best not to think about things sometimes, just do them.'

We half-ran to the shed. The door was already open. I strode inside, the way teachers do when they think someone has done something wrong. The heater was still whirring away.

'It's like a sauna in here,' I said. Sarah and I exchanged relieved glances. Then I saw what he'd done to my shed. My cycling trophy lay on its side in the corner, while my magazines were strewn all over the place. My mum would go mad if she thought I'd left the shed like this.

'Look at the mess he's made,' I said. We both started piling up the cycling magazines again. 'And I had them in order too. It'll take me ages to sort them out now.'

'It's just so stupid of him to do this,' said Sarah. 'I don't understand him, especially as Mrs Porter said he was such a nice, quiet boy.'

'Being dead has certainly changed his personality for the worse,' I said.

'Maybe he's jealous of you.'

'Hmm.' I rather liked the idea.

'I mean, I think it's quite significant that it was your cycling trophy and magazines that he threw about.'

'You could be right. Well he won't be winning any more trophies now.' For a moment I felt quite triumphant. But then I added, 'Still, he'll be back, won't he?'

'I'm sure he will.'

'He probably really enjoys scaring me, makes him feel all powerful when really . . .' I stopped.

Sarah gave me a puzzled look. 'What?'

'You said ghosts haven't got any reflection, didn't you?'

'That's right.'

'So actually they're nothing. Ghosts are just

113

shadows aren't they? Nothing else. And they can't do anything to you, can they? All right, they can make the atmosphere turn cold and throw a few things about – but that's all, isn't it? That's why ghosts are always creeping about at night when you're on your own. I mean, my ghost won't slip into a chair when I'm with Mum or Rachel, will he?'

'What are you getting at?' asked Sarah.

'I'm saying that ghosts are just an illusion really. In a crowd in daylight they wouldn't be any scarier than a moth. That's why they pick their moments and they know that.' I paused. 'They know that fear always feeds upon itself.'

'Where did you read that?'

'I don't know, but it's quite good, isn't it?' I got up. 'Look, Sarah, next time that ghost appears I'll be ready for him.'

Sarah's eyes grew wide. 'What do you mean?'

I hesitated. 'I don't know. I'll challenge him to an arm wrestle or something.'

'What?'

'I'll show him he can't scare me. Then he'll fly off and find some other poor person to bother.'

Sarah looked doubtful. 'I don't think you should do anything until I'm here. After all, as far as ghosts are concerned you are a total amateur . . .'

'But if I don't do something, Sarah, this haunting could go on for weeks . . . even years.'

'But you mustn't challenge the ghost or do anything until I'm here,' she said, staring intently at me.

'Why?'

'It could be very dangerous – for you. Now promise me you won't do anything.'

'All right, Sarah, I promise,' I said.

But I crossed my fingers when I said it.

CHAPTER ELEVEN

That night I woke up, freezing. My duvet must have slipped off again. It was always doing that. I stretched my hand out. The duvet was there. It hadn't moved.

Then I knew.

My enemy was back.

My heart went thump, thump, thump. I tried to steady myself by making out all the familiar shapes in my room. There was my desk with my little television on top of it, above that I could see my model aeroplanes. Next there was my little wooden chair.

My heart stopped.

There was someone sitting on that chair. I could see him. A dark silhouette. Then I remembered. I must have slung my clothes over the chair. I must have been tired. Those clothes had caught me out before. But not this time.

'Alfie.' That voice again. It sounded very near. Where was he?

I swallowed hard. I mustn't let him scare me. Otherwise he'd win again.

'Yeah, what do you want?' I called back. My voice sounded thin and scratchy. But it began to gather power as I went on. 'You think you're scaring me but you're not. I've coughed up scarier things than you.'

I began to laugh contemptuously. My heart was pounding furiously. Sarah had said I mustn't challenge him. But I had no choice. You've got to stand up to bullies. And that's all he was.

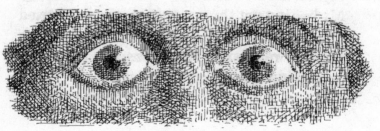

'Come on then, show yourself. Stop hiding in the shadows,' I demanded. As soon as I switch on the light you'll disappear into whatever darkness you've come from. Well I'm going to put the light on right now. So prepare to vanish.'

I stumbled out of bed. My legs felt very wobbly, as if I'd been ill in bed for days. But I was determined. I walked over to the switch. Then I stopped. And my whole body shook, as a memory rushed through me.

I'd hung my clothes up in the wardrobe tonight. Mum had come in and insisted. She said it stopped the clothes from smelling stale. She said . . . never mind what she said.

There was someone sitting on my chair.

The shape stirred. I saw the green uniform. I saw the pale white face. I heard him say, *'Danger.'* Only his voice sounded really close now, as if he was whispering the word in my ear.

'Danger.' He said it again. He was taunting me, mocking me.

That's when something in me snapped. I leaped forward and swung a punch at him. I punched him smack on the face.

And my hand didn't go through him. I

touched something solid, and icy cold.

I pulled my hand back. It stung a little. I was staring into emptiness. I started yelling. 'And if you come back I'll punch you again. Have you got that? You're not wanted here . . .'

I switched the light on. Then I started in horror. In the mirror was a horrible face, all twisted with anger and fear.

It was my face, and it scared me. It didn't look like me. I switched the light off again, scrambled into bed, pulling the cold sheets around me. I felt ashamed of myself for getting so mad. I'd done something wrong tonight and I had a feeling I would pay dearly for it.

But in the morning I felt differently. I'd had to attack the ghost. He was a monster. He'd left me no choice.

Now he'd gone into the darkness, never to be seen again.

It was all over.

I'd defeated him.

CHAPTER TWELVE

Next day I told Sarah what had happened.

It was Friday afternoon and we were taking Molly for a walk. Each day she managed to go a little further.

'No sign of the ghost yet?' asked Sarah. Then she answered her own question. 'He might wait a while before he returns again.'

'Actually, I saw the ghost last night,' I replied, enjoying the look of amazement on Sarah's face.

Then I told her what had happened. We

stopped walking. We stood at the top of Grandad's road. Sarah didn't say a word. She was listening really intently. I could hear her breathing. Then I told her about me punching the ghost, and she sighed loudly.

'You promised you wouldn't do anything until I was there,' she said.

'I know.' I nearly added that I'd crossed my fingers at the time, but I didn't.

'And you shouldn't have punched him. That's so typical of a boy. Now you've just got him mad. He won't give you a minute's peace.'

'Won't he?'

'No. You'll probably find he keeps switching things on and off in your room tonight. Like lights and televisions . . . anything electrical. Ghosts often do that when they're really angry.'

I tried to look as if I wasn't too bothered. 'I'll just switch the telly back on and punch him in the face again.'

'No, you mustn't do that,' cried Sarah in such a high voice that Molly obviously thought Sarah was talking to her and started barking excitedly. Sarah bent down and let Molly lick her ear. 'I really wish I wasn't going off,' she said.

'You smell all right to me.'

Sarah didn't even pretend to smile. She had to go away with her parents for the weekend. 'Now you mustn't do anything else to antagonize the ghost. Just wait until I get back. Do you understand?' She sounded like a teacher speaking to a particularly dense pupil. Then she started scribbling in her notebook. She tore out a page. 'Here's the phone number of where I'll be. Ring me anytime.' Sarah said she would be back by five o'clock on Sunday. I promised to go round and give her a full report.

And at five o'clock on Sunday she was waiting outside her house for me.

'My parents are prowling about,' she said, 'so I thought it might be easier if we talked out here.' We sat on her wall. She looked a bit tense. But I had good news for her. Nothing had happened. He didn't whisper my name, sit in my chair, move anything about – or switch on my television.

123

'I really think he's gone,' I said, finally.

Sarah didn't look as pleased as I'd expected. In fact she almost seemed disappointed. 'He could still come back,' she said.

'I don't think so.' I couldn't resist adding, 'I scared him off. I gave him quite a hard punch, you know. He knows I won't take any more of his nonsense, so he's slunk off. I wish he'd told me where my jacket was, but otherwise I feel pretty pleased with myself. I can get on with the important things – like training for the cycling race.'

A look of horror crossed Sarah's face. 'You're not still doing that?'

'Yeah, why not?'

'But you can't!' exclaimed Sarah. 'You are in danger on that day.'

Now Sarah was starting up all this rubbish about me being in danger. She went on. 'Your time-twin met his doom in a cycling race exactly thirty years ago – everything points to it happening again.'

'For the eight millionth time,' I said, 'he's not my time-twin. And he's gone now.'

'We don't know he's gone for good.'

'I do,' I replied firmly.

'Maybe he's waiting until the day of the race and then he'll suddenly jump out and then you'll lose your balance and go hurtling off your bike . . .'

I jumped up. 'I'm not listening to any more of this.'

'All right then,' said Sarah. 'Do what you like. Go off and meet your doom. But I'm not helping you any more.'

'You didn't help much anyway,' I snapped. 'You might have read all the books, but it was me who got rid of the ghost. Not you.'

She didn't say another word, just stormed off back to her house. I heard her slam the door. I didn't go round to see Grandad and Molly as I'd planned. Instead, I set off on my bike. I cycled around for hours.

Over the next days Sarah and I never spoke. It was a bit petty, I know, but I was still very annoyed with her. She wasn't in charge of me. She couldn't tell me what to do. She didn't know everything.

We took Molly for walks separately and I tried to visit Grandad when she wasn't there.

Grandad noticed something was wrong. I knew he would. I was brushing Molly – I brush her every day – when Grandad said, 'What's up?'

I pretended I didn't know what he was talking about.

'You and young Sarah. Have you fallen out?'

I shrugged my shoulders. I didn't want to talk about it, even with Grandad. But he kept on staring at me, just like Molly does when she wants something.

'I don't know what's wrong.' I shrugged again. 'And I'm not bothered.'

'Of course you are,' said Grandad. 'She's your friend, isn't she?'

I should have said of course she isn't. No-one likes her. She's the Smurf. But I didn't say any of that. I didn't say anything at all.

'Good friends are worth keeping,' said Grandad. But then he changed the subject.

That's one thing about Grandad – he doesn't go on and on about things. He would be seeing

me off at the cycle race on Saturday. He and
Molly. Mum couldn't make it as she and
Rachel were going to my cousin's wedding.
They'd wanted me to go too – as a pageboy.
That's the sort of thing you do when you're
about two months old. I was far, far too old.
Even if I hadn't been in the race I'd have
missed the wedding after hearing that.

The night before the race Sarah spoke to me:
the first time for five days. We were in
Grandad's kitchen. I was at the sink filling up
Molly's bowl with water.

'Are you still going through with the race,
then?' she asked my back.

I whirled round. I was amazed by the question. 'Of course I am.' She immediately started
walking away. 'Look, Sarah, if I pull out then
the ghost's still beaten me, hasn't he?' I called
after her, 'Sarah, wait.'

But she just went on walking away.

Still, tomorrow when I walk in here, as right as rain, she'll have to say something then.

I'd settle for, 'Sorry, Alfie, you were completely right, as always.'

CHAPTER THIRTEEN

And then it was the day of the bike race. I woke up early. I lay in bed listening to the rain pattering against the window.

I could hear Mum and Rachel talking. They were in Rachel's bedroom. Mum's voice was low and reassuring. Rachel was getting in a flap about this wedding. I knew she would. She gets in a flap about everything. If she loses her hairbrush it's a major catastrophe.

Unlike me. This was the day I was supposed to meet my doom, yet I was calm. Sort of. I stomped into the bathroom. I started whistling. 'Stop making that terrible noise,' called my sister. 'You're giving me a headache.'

I whistled even louder. Downstairs Mum was cooking us a 'proper breakfast' – kippers. I started eating. But I wasn't as hungry as I'd expected.

Then from upstairs came a terrible wail. Mum rushed to the bottom of the stairs. 'Whatever's happened?'

'Nothing, except I can't go to the wedding,' cried Rachel.

'Why ever not?'

'I thought I'd mix up my pink glittery and my purple glittery nail polish and make my own colour but it's all gone wrong, and . . . .' her voice became positively tragic, 'I've run out of nail polish remover.'

'Don't panic,' said Mum, 'I'm sure I've got some, somewhere.' She tore upstairs while I went on picking at my kipper.

A short while later I heard them come downstairs again. 'Problem solved,' said Mum, breezing back into the kitchen.

I didn't look up. I didn't want to see my sister. Smelling her was bad enough.

'What a pong,' I said. 'You stink of nail polish.'

'Don't be silly,' said Mum briskly. 'Now, Rachel, you've got to eat something before we go to the hairdresser's. I insist. And – oh Alfie – you must be giving that kipper an inferiority complex. You've hardly touched it.'

'Yes I have,' I lied.

'Not nervous about this race, are you?'

'Of course not.'

'I'm sorry to miss seeing you off.'

'Don't worry about it.'

Mum smiled at me. 'But I'm looking forward to hearing all about it – and that reminds me – Rachel's staying on for the disco but I should be back by four o'clock at the latest, but just in case I'm delayed here's a key. Look after it, as it's my only spare . . .'

'Mum, what are you doing?' interrupted Rachel. 'You know he'll lose it.'

'No I won't,' I hissed fiercely. 'I never lose things.'

'What about your new jacket then?' she said. 'You lost that a while ago.'

'Oh go eat your nail polish,' I muttered.

Her voice rose. 'Honestly, Mum, if he loses that key we'll have to change all the locks and we just can't afford to do that.'

I gave her one of my filthiest stares then beamed at Mum. 'You know you can trust me.'

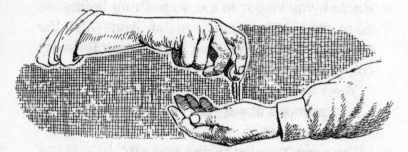

'Yes, I'm sure I can,' said Mum. She handed me the front doorkey to the accompaniment of much head shaking from Rachel. I liked having it. I should always have a key, really.

It was still drizzling with rain when I set off on my mountain bike. Dad had paid for it. I'd chosen this bike because of its colour – red (Manchester United's colour). Only everyone – and especially Mike – went on and on about how my bike was more pink than red. In the end they turned me against the colour. I borrowed Grandad's Stanley knife and peeled off all the red (or pink) on the brake cables. It came off quite easily. Unfortunately there was mainly rust underneath. My mum went mad when she saw what I'd done. But I decided I'd made my bike look more individual.

We were meeting at the church. There was a big banner over the gate. Masses of people were there already including just about everyone from my form, and Crumble. I pretended not to see him. This was a Saturday. He was nothing to do with me today. Mike rode over to me. 'I got my new mountain bike,' he said. 'What do you think?'

'It looks pretty safe.'

'It is.' He went on boasting about how many gears it had. Then he laughed. 'You might at least paint yours. At the moment it's just like the skeleton of a bike.' Mike must have seen my face change for he started to backtrack. 'Still it's certainly different, I suppose.'

But I wasn't insulted. I just wish he hadn't used the word skeleton. Not today.

'Anyway, I've got some mates saving me a place in the front row,' said Mike. 'See you.' I was glad to see him go. He was annoying me.

I spotted Grandad with Molly. There was a

small crowd around them – or rather Molly. When she saw me Molly yelped excitedly. Grandad wished me luck. Then he exclaimed, 'I don't believe it!'

'What?'

He pointed. I didn't believe it either.

Sarah was wobbling towards us on what was undoubtedly the most awful bike I'd ever seen in my life. It even – and you won't believe this – had a basket at the front.

'This is a surprise,' declared Grandad.

Sarah couldn't reply at first; she was so out of breath. Riding that bike was probably the most exercise she'd had for years.

'What are you doing here?' I demanded.

'I've a perfect right to be here,' she snapped.

'Yes, but your bike – is it your mum's or your gran's?' Already people were sniggering at her. Even one or two of the parents were having a discreet chuckle. 'You've made a right show of yourself,' I said. Sarah just ignored me and bent down to pat Molly.

The vicar started nattering through a megaphone, so Grandad and Molly wished us luck again and then they joined the other onlookers at the side. But I went on questioning Sarah. 'You hate cycling. You told me that. So come

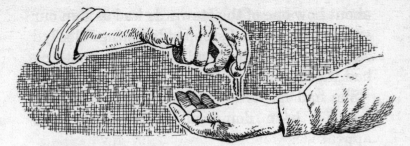

on, what's going on?'

'Mind your own business.'

'And what have you got in that basket, your mum's vegetables?'

I peered down to take a closer look. I saw a small green box with a red cross on it.

'A first-aid kit,' I exclaimed. 'But what . . . ?' I didn't need to say any more. Sarah had gone bright red. 'Is that for my benefit?' I demanded.

She didn't answer, just hunched her shoulders up.

'You're trying to wind me up, aren't you?'

'Look, just ignore me,' she said. 'Act as if I'm not here.'

'Don't worry, I will.'

I turned and faced the vicar who was introducing the stewards now: six guys in yellow jackets, who we'd see along the route to Westlake Park. The vicar was droning on about how one of the stewards had to sign our sponsorship form. I stopped listening. I looked again at Sarah. She really believed something bad was going to happen to me.

She had no right thinking that, unnerving me. I'd been doing all right until she'd appeared.

I sat on my bike lost in my own anger until I noticed something was happening. The race had started.

Mike was already way out of sight. So were half the other cyclists.

I shrugged my shoulders.

'I'm only here for a good laugh,' I announced to no-one in particular.

I decided to just try and enjoy myself. At least I know the route to Westlake Park well. More cyclists whizzed past me. I felt a bit lonely to tell the truth.

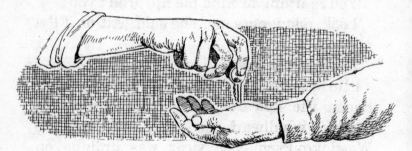

I wondered where Sarah was. Not that I wanted to talk to her. I stared around. I couldn't see her at all at first. Then I saw her, way, way at the back. She had both hands clasped on to the handlebars. She looked so uncomfortable I laughed out loud.

Then she started swerving about. She was going far too close to the kerb. She'd fall off that bike if she wasn't careful. Then she'd need the first-aid kit, not me.

I laughed again, then called out, 'Come out a bit more and try and keep in a straight line.'

She puffed towards me. Her eyes had gone all glassy. 'Don't worry about me; you go off and win the race.'

'No chance now,' I said.

'Are you blaming me?' she demanded.

'To be honest, I think me winning that trophy was a bit of a freak. Most of those cyclists are miles better than me.'

'Oh.' Her voice was a bit gentler. 'Well, goodbye then.'

She wobbled off. I followed her. She came to a corner. 'Put your hand out – signal you're going left.' I put my hand out but Sarah's never left the handlebars. 'What are you doing – why didn't you signal?' I cried.

'Well, I thought I'd leave signalling for today.'

'You can't leave it,' I spluttered. 'I can see I'm going to have to watch you.'

'Don't be silly,' she replied. But from then on we cycled together. We didn't say much, though. Then we passed one of the stewards: 'Frizzle Wood just ahead,' he said. 'Keep going'.

'Now Frizzle Wood, that's great,' I said. 'I often cycle through there.' I turned into a tour guide pointing out that it stretched on for two miles and took us out near the park. I started pointing out interesting things: 'That oak tree over there,' I said, 'is the biggest tree in Frizzle Wood.' I glanced idly at one of its branches.

I couldn't believe what I saw. My bike screeched to a halt.

Sarah ran straight into me.

'You shouldn't have stopped like that,' she exclaimed. 'Even I know that.'

It took a few moments to find my voice. Finally, in a kind of daze I turned round. 'Sarah, hanging from that branch over there . . . is a hand.'

CHAPTER FOURTEEN

Sarah's mouth opened and closed faster than any goldfish's.

'What did you say?'

'Look!' I couldn't stop trembling but she saw where I was pointing all right. On one of the bottom branches a hand was swinging gently in the breeze.

'But what's it doing there?' gasped Sarah.

'Well it's not growing there, that's for sure . . . his other hand is probably somewhere nearby. In fact, there'll be bits of him scattered all over this wood.'

'Ugh, don't. Anyway, how do you know it's a man's hand? It could be a woman's.'

'We've wandered into something very serious. We'd better go and tell someone – now.'

To be honest I didn't want to stay here another second. This wood was suddenly full of danger. The madman who'd done this could jump out at us at any second, eager to add our hands to his collection.

It was in this wood I'd meet my doom. That idea just popped into my head. I couldn't get it to leave.

I was all set to make a sharp exit when, to my amazement, Sarah got down off her bike. She scrambled past me.

'Sarah, what are you . . . ?' I began. Then, with a thud of horror I realized what she was going to do. 'Don't touch the dead man's hand!' I yelled. 'That's evidence.' I leapt off my bike and promptly tripped over. It wasn't my fault. This old tree root or whatever it was got in my way. I scrambled to my feet, trying to look as if I'd meant to do that. Anyway, I was too late; she had pulled the hand down from the branch. She was actually touching it.

I gaped at her in horror.

'Would you like me to perform a magic trick?' she asked.

It's the shock, I thought. It's turned her brain.

'With one swish, Alfie, I can turn the dead man's hand into a . . . Marigold.'

Moments later I was staring down at a pink washing-up glove and feeling distinctly stupid. 'You must admit, from a distance and turned inside out . . . well, even Your Majesty was fooled at first.'

'Only for a micro-second,' said Sarah. 'You see, I used my superior brain power.'

'Just a shame your superior brain power doesn't make you a better cyclist, isn't it?'

Sarah threw the Marigold at me. 'I thought you might want to keep it as evidence.'

'You're so funny.' I said. 'We used to blow these gloves up, you know, to make them look like cows' udders.'

'Yes, I could imagine you doing that,' replied Sarah. But she didn't say it in her usual looking-down-her-nose-at-you way.

I hung the Marigold back on the branch. 'I'll leave it here to scare someone else. And I bet it will, too. Come on then, we must go. We're supposed to be in a race. I wonder if we're last.'

We were. In fact, we reached the park just as the vicar was handing out the trophies. He'd already presented the first and second prizes. He was giving the third prize to Michael, of all people.

I made a face as if I'd just swallowed something very bitter. Sarah saw me. 'If it hadn't been for me you'd have been up there with the winners,' she said. I knew that wasn't true, but I nodded in agreement anyway.

A little group started clapping Sarah and me. Only they were clapping really slowly. Others joined in.

'They're all mocking us,' whispered Sarah. 'I hate them.'

'Stay cool and don't let them see you're upset,' I whispered back. 'Just act as if you're lapping it up.'

I put a big smile on my face, called out, 'Cheers, lads,' and waved at everyone. To my surprise, Sarah gave out some pretty regal waves too.

Afterwards I said loudly to the vicar, 'We figured if we couldn't come first we'd come last. No point in coming in the middle, is there? So where's our prize then?'

The vicar didn't know what to say; he just chuckled nervously. Mike came over waving his trophy under my nose. While he was talking he kept raising his eyebrows and giving me these looks: half-puzzled, half-amused. He wanted to know what I was doing with the Smurf. Sarah must have seen him. The next thing I knew she'd gone.

I saw her standing by the refreshment tent. Everyone was jostling about laughing and talking. Except Sarah. I kept watching her. I was sure she'd take one of those little paper plates and fill it up with food. But she didn't. She just stood there. No-one spoke to her. No-one even seemed to notice her. I thought, she'll slip off home soon.

Then I realized something funny: I didn't want her to go home.

I pushed my way over to the refreshment tent. I grabbed two paper plates right away and piled on as much food as I could on each one. Then I found Sarah. She was still standing on the edge of the refreshment area.

'You're hungry,' she quipped, when she saw me with two plates of food. I didn't actually look at her. I just pointed one of the plates in her direction.

'Is that for me?' She seemed amazed as if I was giving her a plateful of money. 'But I'm not hungry.'

'Go on, take it,' I muttered. She did, and just about scoffed the lot.

Then she told me she'd never been to the park before. I couldn't believe that. So I showed her round. We stayed until it started to rain again.

It was after three o'clock when we set off home.

'You want to get yourself a proper bike, Sarah,' I said.

'I like this one.'

'Behave.'

'I think having a basket is very useful.'

I shook my head. 'You're crazy.'

'So are you.'

'That's true . . . shame you never got a chance to use your first-aid kit, isn't it?' Her face reddened. 'No sign of the ghost today.' Sarah didn't say anything, just went even redder. I couldn't help rubbing it in. 'Just think, if I hadn't punched that ghost he'd still be here now messing about, causing more chaos.'

'You still shouldn't have done it,' said Sarah.

'Can't admit you're wrong, can you?'

'That's because I'm not,' said Sarah, tossing her head defiantly.

I laughed mockingly. After which I decided I'd done enough crowing for now – and changed the subject.

By the time we reached my house the rain was falling really heavily. 'Do you want to

145

come in for a Coke . . . then when the rain's stopped we can go round Grandad's?'

Sarah looked surprised at the invitation, then she actually gave me a tiny smile.

'No-one's at home, but I've got a key,' I said, airily. I dug into my pocket. I felt for the key.

It wasn't there.

'The key's gone!' I cried. 'My mum'll kill me.'

I could already see my mum's anxious, disappointed face. And my sister just gloating with pleasure. 'I've got to find it, Sarah,' I said. 'But it could be anywhere. It must be back at the park.'

Sarah considered. 'No, it'll be nearer than that. You probably lost it when you fell off your bike.'

'I didn't fall off my bike,' I replied indignantly. 'But you could be right. It's probably just by the dead man's hand. Anyway, I'd better go. I'll give you a ring when I get back.'

'I'm coming with you,' said Sarah.

'But you hate cycling.'

'That's true, but four eyes are better than two, aren't they? We'll find it all right.'

'We'd better,' I replied.

CHAPTER FIFTEEN

The moment we set off the weather turned nasty. That's how it seemed anyway. The wind certainly picked up, driving the rain straight into our faces. I wanted to close my eyes. But I daren't. It was hard enough seeing anything with my eyes open.

This was a bad time for a journey. I wouldn't have set out at all if it hadn't been for Rachel. I just couldn't face her if I'd lost the key. I'd rather leave home.

This was all her fault.

Sarah was crouched over the handlebars, gasping every time the rain smacked her in the face.

'Soon be at Frizzle Wood now,' I called. But the wind whipped my words away.

Then I nearly missed the turning. We swerved into it, earning an irate purp from a car.

'I can't believe how dark it's got in the wood,' said Sarah.

I nodded in agreement. I felt as if we were going down a long tunnel. 'We'll probably see more on foot,' I suggested. We clambered off our bikes and squelched our way through the mud. There were massive puddles every-where.

Was my key drowning in one of them? It had to be.

Low-lying clouds circled above us. The wind made the trees rattle and shake.

'Look out for the old oak tree,' I cried to Sarah. And before I'd finished speaking I spotted it in the distance. Something else, too.

The dead man's hand.

Only this time it seemed to be waving at us, urging us forward.

'There it is,' I cried. I felt excited, hopeful.

148

'The key's got to be there. Come on.'

'You go on ahead,' croaked Sarah. 'I'll catch you up.' Rain was dripping off her. She looked as if she was about to fall down.

'Yeah, sure,' I replied, sloshing towards the tree. Then I crouched down. I felt like an explorer searching for a very rare creature. Where was it? I squinted up my eyes.

Out of nowhere came this blast of cold air. It was just as if someone had opened a giant freezer. I could feel it pouring on to my neck. Then something came crashing down on my left shoulder. An icy hand. The next moment another hand gripped my right shoulder. This felt so cold I yelled out. I tried to turn round. I couldn't move. Someone was stopping me.

I couldn't see anyone.

Yet someone was there all right.

It was him.

I struggled frantically, getting more and

more desperate. But I couldn't move. I was caught in some kind of invisible trap. I'd have to stay like this until he decided to let me go.

I let out another cry. I was terrified. All at once Sarah's face loomed up next to mine. Her eyes were like saucers.

'What's happened, Alfie?' she gasped.

'I can't move. It's holding me back.'

'What is?'

'He is. The ghost's here,' I began. Then I let out another cry. Two chilled hands were pressing down even harder on my shoulders now. 'It's come to get me, Sarah,' I gasped, 'just like you said. Run away before it gets you.'

'No, I can't leave you like this,' she began. 'Look, I'll pull it off you.'

She bent down beside me. She was breathing really hard, as if she'd just been running in a race.

I was ice-cold from head to toe now. 'I don't

think you can do a thing,' I began, my teeth chattering, 'but try, anyway.'

'Of course I will,' she began. But before she could do anything there came this great, blinding flash of light. The shock of it made us both fall back on to the mud. I'd always thought lightning was white. But this was electric blue and brighter than the sun. It came racing across the sky. I could see it stretching and growing before it shot down the oak tree: a jagged line of blue fire. There was a great shower of sparks. All at once the earth around us began to shake. Then came this tremendous crack of thunder. The noise ripped through my eardrums while everything around me seemed to be spinning.

I grabbed hold of Sarah's hand or she grabbed hold of mine. I don't remember exactly. And it was hard to make out anything because these little silver flashes kept jumping about in front of my eyes. It was like my own private firework display. I had this prickling sensation. My hair was standing on end.

Then I heard these crackling sounds. They were all around us. It was like hundreds of gunshots going off all at once. Leaves and branches were shooting everywhere; Sarah let go of my hand. I twisted my head round. She was shaking.

'Are you all right?' she asked.

'Yes, I think so.' I suddenly realized I could move my neck again. It ached like crazy, though. 'How about you?'

'Oh, I'm OK,' she said. She'd wrapped both her arms around herself but she was still shaking.

I said, 'I feel like I'm in a war zone somewhere, with guns going off all around me.'

'That's just the branches hitting the ground.'

'I know,' I said quickly. I sniffed. I could smell burning. 'I don't think we're in exactly the safest spot here, do you? We should go.'

'Yes,' agreed Sarah. 'Only my bones feel very heavy at the moment.'

'That's OK,' I said. 'My bones feel pretty heavy too.' There was silence for several moments. Finally, I said, 'I suppose if I'd been under the tree I'd be burnt to a crisp now, wouldn't I?'

'You certainly would.'

'Only he stopped me. I could feel him pressing dead hard on my shoulders, like he was pulling me back. He's got a mighty strong grip for a ghost.' I gave a scratchy kind of laugh. 'He did it, Sarah, he saved me . . . but why?'

She gave an exasperated sigh: the kind contestants on game shows give when they've made a silly mistake. 'I should have realized,' she murmured.

'Realized what?'

She went into her sighing routine again, then she said softly, 'But he's your time-twin.'

'So?'

'So he knew you were in danger. Don't you see, he crossed another dimension to try and warn you.'

A shiver ran through me. 'Only Alfred couldn't get me to understand and I punched him in the face. I really thought he'd vanished for good then.'

'But he was there at your side all the time,' said Sarah. 'You just never knew it.'

There was another rumble of thunder, but it

was a pretty distant one. The thunder was far away now. And Alfred, was he far away now too?

At last we hauled ourselves up out of the mud. My trousers clung to me like freshly hung wallpaper. The rain was stopping and there was this deathly hush. Not a bird for miles around.

This massive, great burn mark was grooved all the way down the oak tree. It was as if it had been split in two.

I thought again of what would have happened to me if I'd been underneath that tree. I stared down at all the dead branches and leaves. They lay everywhere, like the casualties of a battle.

'In the end,' said Sarah, as if reading my thoughts, 'all those branches and leaves will melt into the earth to feed new trees.' Then she sprang forward. There, splattered with mud, was the dead man's hand. She crouched down. Surely she wasn't going to pick it up, I thought. But she'd spotted something else lying beside it. She held it up triumphantly. 'This is your key, isn't it?'

'It has to be,' I said. 'Will you keep hold of it?'

'Yes, it'll be safe with me.'

I shook my head. 'What a day. Now all we've got to do is get back before my mum. She'll go ape if she sees us like this. You can borrow some of my sister's clothes,' I went on.

'Won't she mind?'

'She won't even notice. She's got two wardrobes full of them. Some dresses she only wears once . . . so you might as well use them.'

'Well it would be handy if I could borrow something. My mum would only worry if she saw me like this.'

We fell on to our bikes. How we got home I don't know. But we did – just as Mum was drawing up in her car.

CHAPTER SIXTEEN

Mum looked at us as if she couldn't believe what she was seeing.

'But what are you doing out in the rain? The race finished hours ago – and why are you both covered in mud?'

Sarah and I just hung our heads in reply.

'And Sarah, I'm really surprised at you,' exclaimed Mum. 'I thought you were sensible.' Sarah's head was so low now it was almost touching the ground. 'Well, you can't go home like that. Your mum would have a fit.'

Mum bundled us both inside. She sent Sarah upstairs to have a bath. I had to wait down-stairs in my dressing-gown, while Mum had another go at me. 'Honestly, Alfie, you could both have caught your death of cold. You just don't think, do you? And if you get ill who'll have to stay at home and look after you? Me. That's who.' She stopped. She looked at me a bit more gently. 'What happened, then?'

'Nothing.'

'But when I saw you, you both looked scared out of your wits.'

'So we were, we were scared of you, Mum.'

'Oh, come on.'

I smiled a half-smile. 'You wouldn't believe me, Mum,' I murmured.

'What's that?'

I looked up. 'We just forgot about the time, that's all.'

'I see,' said Mum in a tone which suggested she didn't. 'By the way, in all the fuss, I forgot

to ask how you got on in the race?'

I gave another half-smile. 'We came last, actually.'

Next it was my turn to have a bath. I sat staring out of the window thinking about all that had happened.

Afterwards I saw Sarah in the hallway; she'd just been ringing her mum. She looked funny, as she was wearing one of my sister's old jerseys and a pair of my jeans. I really wanted to talk to her. But I couldn't, not with my mum buzzing about.

Mum had cooked us a meal. Neither of us could eat much. I still felt churned up inside. Then the doorbell rang twice. It sounded urgent.

It was Grandad with Molly. I heard him say to Mum: 'Come on, we're going for a walk.' Grandad sounded really excited.

'But it's raining, Dad,' replied Mum.

'Oh, it's stopped now. So come on, stir your stumps, I've got a surprise for you all. Or rather Molly has.'

He breezed past Mum and put his head round the kitchen door: 'Oh good, Sarah is here too,' he rubbed his hands together. 'That's just perfect.'

Mum joined him. 'Well, off you go then. I think these two could do with cheering up. But please don't let them get all muddy again – I'll have a pot of tea waiting for when you get back.'

'But you've got to come too,' said Grandad, firmly.

'I have?' Mum looked stunned.

'Yes,' said Grandad. 'Why, you haven't been out with Molly since she got wheels, have you?'

Mum looked guilty. And then she came with us. I kept asking Grandad what he was up to, but he only laughed mysteriously in reply.

Outside felt fresh, as if it had just been washed clean. It was still very windy though, and drops of water fell off the leaves. But Molly bounced along beside us so confident and happy that even Mum noticed the change in her.

'You haven't seen anything yet,' said Grandad.

'Have you taught Molly some new tricks?' I asked.

'Wait and see,' replied Grandad.

I began to feel a bit peeved. Up to now I'd been the one who'd taught Molly all her tricks. What trick had Grandad taught Molly without me?

We reached the common. To my surprise

Grandad let Molly off the lead. She seemed to hesitate. 'It's all right, girl, off you go,' whispered Grandad. She ran off a little way then came right back. A few seconds later she was off again. Then all at once she was tearing around that common barking in delight, just like any other dog.

'Just look at her,' said Sarah proudly.

Grandad gave a deep sigh of satisfaction. 'She can go anywhere now . . . the world's her oyster.'

'You've certainly done wonders with that dog,' said Mum to Grandad.

'Couldn't have done it without those two,' replied Grandad. Sarah and I tried to look modest.

Molly bounded over to us again as if to check we were still there. Then she was off again, only this time she ran right to the edge of the common which led on to the back of the church. The next moment she'd disappeared through the gate and was speeding off into the churchyard.

'Oh, look where she's gone – will you two go and get her?' asked Grandad.

Sarah and I sprinted off after her. I reached Molly first. She was sniffing excitedly around

161

one of the gravestones.

'Molly, here girl.'

But Molly just wagged her tail at me and went on sniffing. She was acting as if she'd found something amazing.

She had.

I saw it hanging over the gravestone.

I rubbed my eyes.

It was still there.

My black bomber jacket.

I crouched down beside it while Molly bounded around me. I still couldn't believe it.

I had to check it really was my jacket.

I opened up the inside pocket on the right side. That was where I'd let Mum sew the cotton label with my name on.

There it was.

ALFIE DRAYTON.

But how had the jacket got here?

I knelt down beside the grave. It was very

neglected. The inscription was blurred. I looked more closely: IN LOVING MEMORY OF ALFRED GODDARD, WHO DIED ON OCTOBER 29TH 1967, AGED TEN YEARS.

'Alfred,' I whispered. 'Of course. You left it here for me, didn't you?' And as I spoke I felt something brush past my face. It was the lightest of touches. It could just have been a little breeze. But I knew it wasn't. It was Alfred. His one last message for me. I thought I understood this one. He was going away now. But I didn't want him to.

'Alfred,' I called. 'Don't go yet.'

But the only reply was Sarah's: 'Your jacket – is that your jacket?' She was out of breath.

'It is. Molly found it.'

'Clever, clever girl,' said Sarah, rubbing Molly's head. 'But how did it get here?'

Then I let Sarah read the inscription on the gravestone. She stared and stared at it.

'Alfred was here, too. I felt him rush past me,' I said at last.

'Is he still here?' asked Sarah eagerly.

'I'm pretty certain he's not. That was what he wanted to tell me. Well he's done what he wanted to do, hasn't he?'

Sarah nodded. 'Poor Alfred, he tried so hard to help you.'

'I know, I know.' I felt a bit defensive. 'But it's hard enough understanding humans sometimes – never mind ghosts.'

'I wonder what Alfred was like when he was alive?' asked Sarah. She didn't wait for me to answer. 'I think Alfred was very shy, you know, and very lonely too.' She turned away, and she was speaking so softly I had to lean forward. 'He was lonely when he was alive, and he still is now. He finds it very hard to communicate – and yet he wants to so much.' Her voice started to shake. 'I wish he'd stayed here a bit longer.'

'I'll miss him as well,' I said. 'Just when I was getting to understand him too. But anyway *I'm* still around.' I gave a kind of laugh. Then I reached out my hand to her. Sarah half-turned round. She looked at me, then took my hand. She held it tightly.

'Hey,' I said, 'you've got nearly as strong a grip as Alfred.'

She gave me one of her flickering smiles. Then we spotted Grandad and Mum coming over to us.

Grandad recognized the name on the tombstone. 'That was the boy Mrs Porter mentioned, wasn't it?'

'Yes, Grandad, it was.' I put the jacket on again. I remembered the smell of it. How big it felt. Then I noticed something else: it was bone-dry.

'But how did it get here?' asked Mum.

'There's a story about all this, isn't there?' said Grandad.

'Quite a long story, actually,' said Sarah.

'I think it's time we heard it, don't you?' said Grandad.

I looked at Sarah. She nodded. We went back to Grandad's. He made us tea and toast, then we sat by the fire and I told the story I've just been telling you. Only Sarah kept interrupting me. But I didn't mind. This was a special story and every bit had to be right.

Mum and Grandad didn't interrupt once. They just sat there, their faces half in shadow. After we'd finished I said, 'And that's our story. So what do you think, do you believe in ghosts now, Grandad?'

Grandad stirred his tea thoughtfully; he hadn't drunk it once while we'd been talking. 'It's a good yarn, I'll give you that.'

'But do you believe it really happened?' asked Sarah.

'I know you two believe it,' said Grandad. He was smiling now.

'But what about you?' I persisted.

Grandad sat back in his chair. 'I'll tell you this; I'd like to believe it was true.'

'Of course it's true Grandad,' I exclaimed. 'If it hadn't been for Alfred I'd be toast now.'

'But I know it's hard for older people to understand things like this,' said Sarah kindly. 'My great-grandad didn't believe men would ever walk on the moon, not even when he saw them on television.'

We turned towards Mum. She didn't say much at all.

But next day we asked Mum if we could borrow the clippers as Sarah and I wanted to get rid of the weeds on Alfred's grave, and to my surprise she came with us. She even stopped off at the florist shop and bought a bunch of chrysanthemums.

Much later I went back to Alfred's grave with Molly. It was grey-dark now and there was no-one about, just a few birds twittering drowsily. I knelt down and Molly snuggled up next to me, her head warm on my knee.

If only Alfred hadn't left so fast. I wondered how far away he was, and whether he could still hear me. Probably not. But just in case, I whispered, 'Alfred, just to let you know, you won't see a single weed on your grave again. Sarah and I will see to that. And . . . I'm really sorry I punched you in the face.'

I got up and Molly and I began to walk away. But then I turned back and called into the darkness, 'I'll never forget what you did for me, Alfred. NEVER.'

THE END

THE GHOST DOG

PETE JOHNSON

'I sensed hot breath on my neck. It was right behind me. It'll get me, I must run faster . . . faster . . .'

Only mad scientists in stories can create monsters, can't they? Not ten-year-old boys like Daniel. Well, not until the night of his spooky party when he and his friends make up a ghost story about a terrifying dog . . . It's a story made up to frighten Aaron – tough, big-headed Aaron. But to Dan's horror, what begins as a story turns into a nightmare. Each night the ghost dog – a bloodthirsty, howling monster – haunts his dreams, and Dan suspects that what he conjured up with his imagination has somehow become . . . real!

A spooky tale filled with chills and thrills, from top children's author Pete Johnson.

WINNER OF THE 1997 YOUNG
TELEGRAPH/FULLY BOOKED AWARD

0 440 86341 4

MY FRIEND'S A WEREWOLF

PETE JOHNSON

Now I know for certain Simon is a werewolf!

Kelly always thought werewolves only existed in
stories and late-night films. Until Simon moves
in next door. Kelly and Simon become instant
friends, but Kelly just can't help noticing that
there's something very odd about her new friend.
For one thing, he wears black gloves all the
time – even at school. And could that be hair
starting to sprout on his face? Last, but
definitely not least, there's the howling at
night . . .

Aren't werewolves . . . dangerous?

'A book to make any reader stop and think'
The School Librarian

0 440 863422

EYES OF THE ALIEN

PETE JOHNSON

Huge dark eyes with no pupils . . .

Sam and Freddie, both fostered with the same family, are best friends. Sam even laughs at Freddie's jokes! But after Sam has an accident and knocks herself unconscious, she begins to have weird nightmares about a sinister figure with huge eyes – *alien* eyes. Freddie, who thinks he knows *everything* there is to know about extra-terrestrials, jokes that aliens must be after Sam – trying to contact her. But it's just his imagination, isn't it?

Until they see the spaceship . . .

A shivery new tale from the author of the award-winning *The Ghost Dog*.

'Pete Johnson has proved himself time and time again to be an author of exceptional talents'
THE SCHOOL LIBRARIAN

ISBN 0 440-86390-2

A CORGI YEARLING ORIGINAL
PAPERBACK

THE MIDNIGHT HAND

PAUL STEWART

Something is out there . . .

At the stroke of midnight, as a huge bronze bell tolls the hours, something stirs in a dark and narrow recess. A hand. A skeletal hand with a monstrous awareness of a long ago tragedy . . .

Tom, newly arrived at Styles Grange boarding school, is awaken on his very first night by the creepy feeling of something stroking his face. Then suddenly, scuttling into the shadows under his bed, is . . . a severed hand!

A bloodcurdling nightmare of a tale from a master of suspense.

0 440 86348 1

THE WAKENING

PAUL STEWART

'One is dead, but not forgotten, a name lived on when the body was rotten . . .'

Sam is scared – more scared than he's ever been before. Each night, when he goes to sleep, he dreams he is going to the same place – a dark, silent forest, choked with dense undergrowth. And then the voices begin . . .

First he hears children chanting – as if they are playing some old game. Then, in the centre of the forest, a hand claws its way out of the ground. Someone – or something – has been brought back to life. What's more, it has come with an astonishing message that Sam cannot afford to ignore . . .

'A tremendous pacy read with short, punchy chapters' *Books for Keeps*

'Totally unputdownable' *The School Librarian*

0 440 86347 3

ROOM 13

ROBERT SWINDELLS

The night before her school trip, Fliss has a terrible nightmare about a dark, sinister house – a house with a ghastly secret in room thirteen. Arriving in Whitby, she discovers that the hotel they will be staying in looks very like the house in the dream. There is one important difference – there is no room thirteen.

Or is there? At the stroke of midnight, something strange happens to the linen cupboard on the dim landing. Something strange is happening to Ellie-May Sunderland too, and Fliss and her friends find themselves drawn into a desperate bid to save her.

WINNER OF THE 1990 CHILDREN'S BOOK AWARD

0 440 862272

CLOCKWORK
or ALL WOUND UP

PHILIP PULLMAN

Tick, Tock, tick, tock! Some stories are like that. Once you've wound them up, nothing will stop them . . .

A tormented apprentice clock-maker – and a deadly knight in armour. A mechanical prince – and the sinister Dr Kalmenius, who some say is the devil . . . Wind up these characters, fit then into a story on cold winter's evening, with the snow swirling down, and suddenly life and the story begin to merge in a peculiarly macabre – and unstoppable – way.

'Exciting, scary, romantic and deliciously readable' THE GUARDIAN

SILVER MEDAL WINNER,
SMARTIES AWARD IN 1997

SHORTLISTED FOR
THE CARNEGIE MEDAL IN 1997

ISBN 0 440-86343-0

Now available from all good bookshops

GHOST ON THE LOOSE

HELEN DUNWOODIE

As she climbed towards the half-landing, Rowan found herself mysteriously compelled to slow down. What was so special about Robert's room that he wouldn't allow anyone else inside it?

For Rowan it is bad enough having to live with Robert, Mum's boring new boyfriend, without his ridiculous obsession with his study. What can he be hiding there that is so important? Or so horrible?

Rowan's not the only one who's intrigued by the study. In fact, there's someone who's discovered Robert's secret and is determined to expose him. The only problem is that Lady Maisie McNeil is a ghost and she can't wreak her revenge without a bit of help from someone in the twentieth century. It looks like she's found just the girl . . .

0 440-86380-5